# MONSTER

---

## MADE & BROKEN II

### NORA ASH

# ONE

EVELYN

I knew I was in trouble when my boss didn't send a regular goon to pick me up.

For the first time since I'd made the mistake of borrowing money from Gerald Brigs, casino owner, mafia boss and all-round scumbag, he came by my flat in person. Not a good sign.

In my one and a half years of service to London's underworld, I'd learned that any deviation from the norm was never good.

"Evelyn. Always a pleasure, my dear," said the man on my doorstep. He was wearing a trench coat and a thin-lipped smile that didn't touch his eyes.

I tried to return the expression, but could only manage a grimace as I swept my gaze over his three companions. The two goons he'd brought as bodyguards I didn't recognize, but the third man I did.

Where Gerald rarely bothered with his lowliest employees, his nephew, Leo, was the guy who usually briefed me on my marks and dealt with any situations the goons couldn't. I'd also witnessed what he did to the prostitutes unfortunate enough to work for the Brigs empire. I made it a point to never be alone in a room with him.

"Have I done something wrong?" I asked. Leo closed the door behind the two, leaving their two-goon escort outside. I mentally reviewed the details of the last assignment they'd given me. I had done everything they'd asked, as I always did. I might not have made it to university, but I was smart enough to know what happened to people who disobeyed a crime lord.

"On the contrary," Gerald said as he took in my studio flat. "You've been doing such an excellent job, we've decided it's time to entrust you with something a bit more... delicate." He reached into his coat and produced a brown A4 envelope.

I took the brief from him, examining its contents. Where normally the envelope would contain a couple of pages' worth of information on the mark, this time there was only a picture and a series of seemingly random words. I held it up, scrutinizing it to see what was so different about this guy.

The first thing I noticed was that he was exceedingly handsome. His black hair was tousled perfectly, though it was obvious it had required no effort on his part. Dark brows framed his gray, almond-shaped eyes and his cheekbones were strong and defined. If his mouth hadn't been so soft, his features would almost have been too prominent to call beautiful. But it was—and he looked like a freaking supermodel.

"Er... are you sure I'm a good match?" I bit my lip, feeling oddly self-conscious under the intensity of the photo's stare. "I mean..."

It wasn't that I was bad-looking. My figure might have been fuller than what was considered the hallmark of conventional beauty, but my curves had lured enough hapless men into Brigs' claws that I knew the appeal of my red hair, round hips, and full breasts. But this guy was clearly a class—or five—above mine. I was distinctly more girl-next-door than swimsuit model.

"I mean, he's probably used to more high society girls," I finally managed, pulling my gaze from the picture to look at my boss.

A small smile pulled on his lips. "You're the perfect girl for this job. His name is Marcus Steel, and he has something of mine. A pen drive. I want you to get an invitation to his flat and find this pen drive for me. It's bound to be somewhere secure, so there's a chance you'll have to get into his safe. The list on there are things and people that might mean something to him. Use that to work out the code."

I blinked down at the list. "How on Earth am I meant to figure out a code to his safe from random words?" I might have plenty of street smart, but solving ciphers was above my pay grade.

Brigs' smile turned cooler. "Don't sell yourself short. We've been nothing but pleased with your results so far—I am certain you won't disappoint me this time, either. After all, such a *delicate* assignment will cut a thousand pounds off your debt rather than the usual five hundred."

His tone made it clear that I didn't want to find out what would happen if I failed. Then the other implied part of the assignment dawned on me and I paled. I had lured men with the promise of my body before, but I'd never had to follow through. Once the poor idiots followed me to the designated drop-off point, Brigs' goons had always taken over. But if I was supposed to get an invitation to this mark's home... then there would be no one to intervene. And a guy like that would most definitely expect sex if he brought a woman home.

It was kind of funny—before Brigs, I would have been more than happy to spend a night with a man that looked like this Marcus Steel, but now... When Brigs had discussed how I could repay my loan, I'd been very adamant I wouldn't work in one of his brothels, which was what landed me my job as a Honey Trap. But deep down, I'd known it would only be a matter of time before they would make me go all the way.

The way Leo treated the other women in his employ, it was pretty obvious no one in the Brigs empire cared about a woman's right to her own body.

I dug my nails into the palm of my free hand. I knew better than to protest. I'd just have to work out how to get out of any sexual obligations once I was inside Marcus Steel's home. I might be forced to work for the mafia, but someday I would be free from them again, and when that day came I wanted to be able to look myself in the eye.

I forced a smile on my face as I looked at my boss. "Okay. I'll get your pen drive back. Where can I find this Marcus Steel?"

# TWO

## EVELYN

*Eleonore* was one of the fanciest clubs I'd ever been to. I picked up my marks at clubs often enough, but they were usually the type with loud dance music and a mixture of drugs and semen lining the bathroom stalls.

When I walked up to *Eleonore,* the red carpet guiding the way to the doors muted the sound of my clicking heels, and instead of jarring dubstep blasting out whenever a patron passed through the double doors, the soft, lilting notes of jazz music wafted into the night.

I smiled hesitantly at the huge bouncer taking up most of the step in front of the door. Even though I'd worn the kind of camouflage that would help me fit in here—a black dress that managed to still look classy, even though it certainly marketed my cleavage nicely—I didn't exactly feel at home. Even when I wasn't working for Brigs, my usual attire consisted of jeans and a t-shirt. Or, of course, my uniform when I worked my day job as a waitress. *Eleonore* managed to make me feel like I was sticking out like a sore thumb before I'd even gotten inside.

But the bouncer simply unclipped the red velvet rope for me, stepping aside as he let me through.

"Thank you," I said as I passed him, offering him a smile as well.

If he heard me, he ignored me. *Well, suit yourself, Grumpy.*

I left my coat with a girl working the wardrobe and continued in through another set of double doors, these ones made from glass with gilded bars functioning as door knobs.

I had to pull myself together to not let my jaw hit my chest at the barrage of impression that washed over me on the other side. At the far corner was a beautiful bar, which looked like it was made from hardwood and polished so perfectly even the soft lighting in the club reflected off it. The plush, deep-red carpet from the entrance and corridor turned to parquet flooring that led to multiple high tables and chairs in front of a small dance floor and a stage. Not many people graced the chairs—it was a Tuesday night, after all—but on the stage a band played the enticing jazz rhythms I'd been able to hear since entering the club.

I soaked in the atmosphere, enjoying the sophisticated ambience as much as the music itself. I'd always loved jazz.

But I was here for a job, and it didn't involve standing around wishing for things to have worked out differently. I sighed, pulling myself out of the revelry.

A quick scan of the few patrons at the tables told me that my mark wasn't among them, nor was he part of one of the two couples slow dancing in front of the stage, seemingly lost to the rest of the world. Thank God. That could have been awkward.

I looked back over at the bar and frowned at the flirting couple near the end closest to me. They were blocking my view of the other side of it, so I decided to walk on over and check it out. If nothing else, a drink was always a good way to calm my nerves before I picked up my mark.

On the other side of the couple, a tall man sat at the very far end, one shoulder leaned against the wall. My heart sped up with a burst of adrenaline. Could it be him? I craned my neck in an effort to see him better, but he was facing away. All I could see was ebony hair and incredibly wide shoulders underneath a black shirt.

"What can I get you, miss?"

I jolted at the unexpected voice and flashed a nervous smile at the barman. Something about the underplayed extravagance set me on edge, as if everyone would be able to tell I came from several rungs down the social ladder.

"Vodka and tonic, thanks," I said, trying to keep my tone indifferent and effortless.

When he grabbed for the bottle of Grey Goose, I had

to bite the inside of my cheek to keep from protesting. Instead, I smiled sweetly when he passed me my drink and added a generous tip. Brigs always covered expenses, and if Tall, Dark, and Mysterious at the end of the bar didn't turn out to be Marcus Steel, then I might need the barman's help to locate him later.

Mustering my courage, I took a quick sip of my drink and then walked over to the seat right next to the guy I was hoping was my mark.

"It's a lovely band," I said as I slid in on the bar stool, somehow managing to get on it relatively gracefully. Being a short girl doesn't make wrangling of bar stools an easy task.

Talk, Dark, and Mysterious didn't so much as spare me a glance.

Maybe he didn't hear me?

"Do you come here often?" Okay, so it was cheesy, but from my experience, it worked.

His only reaction was to take a swig of what looked like cola from his own glass.

Right, then. So he was an arse. I pinched my lips and reminded myself I preferred it that way—my job was better when the guy Brigs had me lure into a trap was a jerk. It made it easier to pretend like he deserved what happened to him after I left him with Brigs' goons.

Emboldened by my annoyance, I skipped past the usual smalltalk and instead slipped my drink-free hand underneath the bar and onto his thigh, letting my finger-tips graze the bulge between them.

The strength of his muscles clenching underneath my touch surprised me—I could *feel* the power in his thigh against my palm and half-expected him to shoot out of his chair.

It wasn't what I'd expected. Surprise, sure, but the deathly silence from my unwilling companion made an eerie sense of foreboding tingle down my spine and raise every hair on my body. Slowly, I looked up, my irritation with his previous lack of response replaced by anxiety.

Marcus Steel's ice-gray eyes met mine when my gaze made it all the way up.

Only the man staring down at me was nothing like his picture. Sure, his ruthless good looks were the same, from the black cascade of tousled hair to the soft lips and defined features, but what was *behind* that icy gaze, the photo hadn't managed to convey. If it had, I would have tried much, much harder to get out of this assignment.

Everything about that look screamed *danger*, making the reptilian part of my brain wake in a shock of adrenaline.

I trembled as every nerve ending strained to its fullest, making my skin so hypersensitive I could feel the warmth radiating from him. The faint trace of his cologne hit my flared nostrils, along with something else. Something unidentifiable that heated the lower parts of my abdomen and made me squeeze my thighs together, even as a primal fear dug its claws in deep.

*Oh.* Maybe "*it*" wasn't so unidentifiable, after all.

There was no doubt in mind, after no more than three seconds' eye contact, that this man was trouble.

But he was also one hundred percent alpha male, and despite the overwhelming sense of peril that rushed over me staring into his eyes, my body was seemingly also perfectly in tune with the *other* aspect of his nature.

The unexpected flood of arousal dampened my initial fear enough that I remembered I probably needed to say something soon.

"Hi," I croaked. Not the smoothest of lines, but given how my hand was still grasping his thigh, too petrified to let go, I figured it was better than nothing.

Marcus didn't respond, and his face remained completely impassive.

"I'm Evelyn Embry," I continued, my voice still not much louder than a hoarse whisper. The second my name left my lips I could have smacked myself. I hadn't meant to give him my real name—it was page-freaking-one in dealing with a mark. But his overwhelming presence had made it slip out without conscious thought, and now there was nothing I could do to take it back. Hopefully, he would have forgotten it before he ever realized my true intentions.

His eyes finally moved then, flicking briefly to my hair,

across my face and—finally—to my amply displayed breasts, where they lingered for just a second before he looked back up again. His gaze made a hot blush follow the path of his eyes, and I couldn't hold back a shaky exhale as I stared into his darkened eyes. His pupils seemed larger, as if the light in the room had dimmed, even though the shine from the polished bar told me otherwise.

"What you're selling, little sister, I'm not buying."

I blinked at the rumbling timbre of his voice. The softness in it completely contradicted everything else about his presence.

"I'm not selling anything."

His eyes briefly landed on my hand on his thigh. My fingertips were still brushing ever so lightly against the bulge of his cock.

"*Oh!* No, I'm not... I'm not a prostitute," I stammered, my blush increasing ten-fold. Yeah, of course he would think the stranger groping him would be looking for a client. *Eleonore* wasn't your run-of-the-mill nightclub— uninvited touching wasn't expected.

This wasn't working out at all like I'd planned. I finally managed to remove my hand from his thigh, placing it awkwardly on the bar between us.

"I just..." I looked up into those glacier-cool eyes and felt all my barriers come crumbling down. How did a single person shake me so thoroughly? I felt naked underneath his stare, and it both frightened and aroused me more than it had any business doing. "I wanted to meet you."

"Why?"

Not the question I'd expect from a guy who looked like Marcus Steel.

"You're the most handsome man I've ever seen." I frowned. "Why do women normally want to meet you?"

His face remained impassive, but the darkness in his eyes intensified, pulling at those warring sensations in my gut: the cold dread of adrenaline, and the hot, champagne fizz of pure sexual attraction. "They don't."

I raised both eyebrows. "I find that really hard to believe."

Finally, he turned away from me, relegating his full focus to his glass as he took a swig. "They're scared of me."

Well, that I could believe. I looked back at my own drink, mulling over my plan of attack. Now that he wasn't staring at me so intensely, I could think clearly again—even if every cell of my body was still keenly aware of his proximity.

"*I* want to know you," I said, glancing out the corner of my eye for a reaction.

Marcus put his glass down, still not looking in my direction.

"You're scared of me, too." The deep rumble in his voice sent shivers up my back. If he knew I was flirting, he wasn't responding. But he wasn't ignoring me, either.

"Yes," I said, deciding honesty was my best course with this man. Gently, I placed my hand back on top of his thigh, a bit lower this time. Again, he tensed at my touch, but not as rigidly as before.

"But that doesn't change the fact that I want you more than I've ever wanted another man in my life." I glanced up at his profile, flustered by the knowledge that this wasn't just a line delivered to ensnare a mark, nor was it a lie. "Maybe that's what scares me."

He looked at me then, and this time, the darkness in his eyes bore the faintest trace of heat. But it wasn't the kind of lust I'd seen in a man's eyes before. It was far more volatile, far more frightening than anything I'd known before, and even the barest hint of his desire set my body aflame with unrivaled *need*.

"No, *Evelyn*. That's not why you're afraid."

"Is it because you'd try to hurt me?" I whispered, my voice breaking.

His nostrils pulled up, a flash of anger mixing with the heat in his gaze. "No."

A breath of relief I hadn't realized I'd been holding rushed out of my lungs. I believed him. I had no idea what it was about him, but something at the very depths of my being knew he wasn't lying. I grasped my drink and downed the rest of the glass in one, burning mouthful. Then I slid off my seat and stood to face him on shaky legs.

"Come."

Despite the minimal movement of his mouth, I recognized his question in the gesture.

"You're taking me to your place." I slipped my hand from his thigh up to his arm, resting it on the soft fabric of his shirt. "And then you'll let me get to know you."

The slightest crease appeared between his dark eyebrows, his gaze flickering to my hand on his arm before he found my eyes once more. The desire in his own was more prominent now, and I had to clench my thighs together to quell the sudden rush of warmth blooming out from between them. God, I wanted him. In that moment, I didn't care about my assignment or Brigs or any of the shit I was mixed up in that'd landed me here. I didn't even care that that barely bridled ferocity in his icy gaze flamed as he looked me over once more, taking in my curves as well as my face.

"You don't know what you're asking for," he rumbled.

"Then show me," I said, swallowing thickly as he stared me down.

Marcus exhaled through his nose. Then, moving as smoothly as a large cat, he got off the chair and held his hand out to me.

Gingerly, I put my palm in his.

When he closed his hand around mine, I knew I would never be the same as I had been before I met Marcus Steel.

# THREE

## MARCUS

*Evelyn Embry.*

She was not meant to be here, not meant to be with *me*.

And yet there she sat, leaning into the passenger seat of my Porsche with her luscious breasts spilling out of her low neckline and the roundness of her thighs easily visible through the tight fabric of her dress.

My cock throbbed, and I fought back a shiver at the memory of her hand grazing against it when she'd so brazenly demanded my attention.

I'd never wanted a woman like I wanted her, from the moment her heat penetrated my trousers and into my skin. It took all I had to not just pull over and fuck her raw on the side of the road, leaned over my car with her dress hiked high around that fine arse of hers.

I clutched at the steering wheel and gritted my teeth.

This was a mistake. I shouldn't have let her into my car, shouldn't have taken her hand when she'd told me I was bringing her home.

I had to pull over right this second and tell her to get out.

But everything in me reeled at the thought, the monster in my chest snarling in defiance. It didn't want to let her go. *I* didn't want to let her go.

Her scent, jasmine and honey and *woman*, permeated the air in my car, filling my nostrils until my cock was so hard it hurt. Everything about her made me burn with a need I'd never experienced before.

*Why are you here, little one?* I looked at her out the corner of my eye, drawn to her like a moth to a flame. Why was she here? She recognized the monster in me; I saw it when she looked into my eyes. She may not have understood *what* she saw, but her body intuited the danger—there was no question about it. And still, she persisted.

It was too late for regrets. Too late to stop, because the moment our eyes locked, the monster had recognized *her*. I had no idea how, or why—why her, why now—but ever since she put her soft little hand on me, I'd been fighting tooth and nail to keep the monster down. Even now, it was roaring to break free and sweep me away in the liberating rush of oblivion I knew all too well.

I should never have taken her with me. I should have turned her down, should have left and not looked back.

I needed to end this, before she was inside my flat. Before the door closed behind us, with no one there but her and me.

I clasped my hands harder around the steering wheel to steady my thrumming pulse at the monster's roar of denial.

*No.*

As I pulled into the parking garage underneath my high-rise apartment block, I knew one thing with absolute certainty: this woman was going to be mine, and there was nothing either of us could do to stop it.

# FOUR

## EVELYN

The car ride to Marcus' flat took place in complete silence, and it was enough for my brain to have regained some measure of control once he opened the door to his penthouse in one of the posher parts of London.

I drew in a deep breath as I stepped past him and over the threshold, catching the scent of his cologne again and that certain something behind it that went straight to my core. It made me shiver, partly from want and partly from the knowledge of what I was about to do.

Marcus Steel was sex on a stick, sure, but he was a lot of other things too. I'd never been in the presence of a human being who could awaken my reptile brain like he did. Gerald Brigs and his nephew might make my skin crawl, but my fear of them stemmed from knowing what they could do to me. With Marcus, it was this unmistakable sense that there was something dark and unbridled right beneath the surface, clawing to be set free.

And here I was, alone with him in his flat. More than willing to be naked and vulnerable underneath him.

I walked further into the apartment and set my purse on the kitchen island, focusing on my surroundings in an attempt at steadying my rampant hormones. As much as I wanted to climb him like a monkey, I needed a moment to collect myself. My body might have been on board with the evening's development, but I was still here on a job.

I looked around for something to distract me—and found it at the far wall. The entire side of the room was made up of floor-to-ceiling windows, offering the most spectacular view of the city I could have ever imagined. Even in the dark, hundreds of thousands of lights from the streets below twinkled like a second set of stars.

"Wow," I breathed, making my way to the glass so I could get the full view. It felt like having the entire city at my feet. "That is some view."

Marcus didn't answer me, but I heard him move further back in the flat. I was too mesmerized by the view to pay him any mind.

I'd known he was wealthy from the jazz club he hung out in, and when he'd led me to his black Porsche it'd been firmly cemented. But this? This was what the one percent lived like. Views like this didn't come below a seven-digit pay grade.

"It feels like everything down there is meaningless—

like it's so far removed, it doesn't matter. It's so... peaceful," I mused, not expecting an answer from my silent companion. Feeling emboldened by the odd sense of calm, I wiggled out of my heels to dig my toes into the plush, luxurious rug that covered the parquet floors underneath a black sofa set. It felt exactly as good as I'd imagined, and I sighed with pleasure and turned to study the rest of the room. I'd been too preoccupied with the amazing view to really pay it much mind.

It was a big, open-plan room consisting of a kitchen by the entrance and a large living room, but it'd been sparsely decorated, the sofa set being the only real furniture in the room, save some bar stools by the kitchen island and a dining table further in.

No decorations adorned the walls either, but when my eyes caught a framed picture by the TV, I did a double take.

A cute baby with dark strands and gray eyes lay sprawled on a lambskin, looking at the camera with a wide smile. The frame was inscribed *August 1, 2015*.

"Is that... your kid?" Imagining Marcus with a child seemed near-impossible, and if the date on the frame was the baby's birth date, then it was only a little more than a year and a half.

"No." It was the first he'd spoken since the club, and the rumble of his voice made me look back at him, heat making its way to my abdomen again.

I raised an eyebrow at him. Who the heck had a

picture of a kid who wasn't theirs as the only decoration in their entire living room? "Whose then?"

"My brother, Blaine's."

Well, that explained the colorings matching Marcus' so much. I squinted at the picture. "Boy or a girl?"

"Boy. His name is Aidan."

Something softened in his voice when he said the baby's name, and when I looked up at him, for a moment it was reflected in his eyes too.

"It's funny, you don't exactly come across as a family man," I said.

"Family's everything."

I thought of my mother, the usual stab of sadness making my heart ache just a little. "Yeah." There wasn't anything I wouldn't do for family—which was why I was in this situation in the first place.

I looked back up at Marcus and my sadness melted away.

The gentleness in his gaze was gone, a dark smolder taking its place.

My body reacted with a delicious shiver, choosing to focus on the obvious lust rather than the danger.

I wanted this—I wanted the raw, untamed parts of him to consume me. I wanted his body against mine, I wanted to taste those luscious lips of his, and to hell with what I'd have to do after.

With a small smile I undid my coat and dropped it on the floor before reaching behind me for my zipper. It came down easily, the sound of it filling the sudden silence in the room.

I felt Marcus' eyes on me like a molten caress as I let go of my dress, letting it pool to the floor at my feet. I might have felt outclassed when we were in the jazz club together, but not now. He didn't say a word, but the electricity of his rapt focus sparked in the air around me, and I knew without a shadow of a doubt that right now, at this moment, there was nothing in this world he wanted as much as he wanted me.

It made me feel powerful.

I reached up to let down my hair from the pinned updo, letting the ginger locks fall around my shoulders and brush the top of my pushed-up breasts. Even though the black lace bra technically still covered them, they were so indecently on display I was sure he'd be able to make out my nipples pebbling as his silent desire fanned my arousal.

I reached behind me again, this time unclasping my bra and letting it fall to the floor on top of my coat. My panties followed, and then I stood naked.

Marcus' shaky exhale made me look back up into his eyes, the beginning of a coy smile on my lips. I was going to suggest he follow my lead, but the look on his face made me pause.

Fear.

He was... scared?

Only then did I notice he'd clutched his hands around

the edge of the kitchen island, and that his knuckles were white from the strength he grasped it with.

"What are you afraid of?" I whispered.

"I want you," he said, his voice gruff from obvious restraint. "Too much."

I cocked my head as I took in his posture and the tight set of his jaw. He looked like a man who was doing everything he could to hold himself back. It made warm excitement trickle down my spine and goosebumps of pleasure rise up along my arms. As far as I was concerned, there was no such thing as being wanted *too much* by him, not right now.

I stepped out of my dress and panties, making sure to sway my hips as I walked toward him until I stood right in front of him. I only came up to his shoulders, and their span easily dwarfed even my curvy body, but this close I could practically *feel* the tension roll off him in waves. That someone as powerful as Marcus Steel was afraid of *me* gave me the confidence I needed to reach up and ghost my palms over his tensed shoulders before I began to unbutton his shirt, one button at a time.

The shaky intake of his breath as my hands skimmed over his hard pecs made me have to hide a smile. Yeah, he was in a bad state. It only made me feel bolder.

Once my fingers undid the last button, his shirt hung open and I had to bite my lip to hold back a gasp of my own. His clothes hadn't been able to hide the shape or size of his powerful body, but the prominence of the stacks of hard, lean muscles underneath was unexpected. Marcus' pecs narrowed down into a bulging row of abs, and just above his belt I could see the start of the pronounced V of his hips.

*Holy cow.*

I mindlessly reached out to let my palms stroke across his smooth body, enjoying the shiver my touch pulled from him. His skin was hot underneath my hands, and when I ghosted across his nipples with the tip of a finger they hardened into tight little points.

My own body responded to his with a flood of moisture. *God,* I needed more.

I reached back up to push the shirt off his shoulders and looked up at his face.

It was still a mask of restraint, but his eyes blazed with desire so hot it nearly set me on fire. Yet still, he wasn't touching me.

Without breaking eye contact I reached back down, brushing down across his abs and the narrow trail of hair below his navel until I got a hold of his belt.

Marcus moved then, one of his large hands wrapping around my wrist. "You don't have to do this."

"I want to." I leaned in and kissed the center of his chest, not releasing my hold on his belt. He shuddered under my lips but held on to my wrist, his fingers spasming as my breath skimmed across his flesh.

"Evelyn..." His deep voice sounded anguished, as if holding back was causing him physical pain.

"Let go," I murmured, before brushing another kiss across his chest, this time right above his left nipple. "I want this. I want *you*. Let go."

He breathed out shakily, letting his hand fall to his side.

My fingers resumed their quest, undoing his belt and then finding the button and zipper of his pants, and all the while I kept my eyes locked in his. Only when I hooked my thumbs in his pants and boxer shorts did I let my gaze slide back down, just in time to see his cock spring free.

*Oh, holy—!*

"*Wow*." I wasn't aware I'd said anything out loud before his amused snort reached my ears, but I was too preoccupied with staring to be embarrassed.

Marcus was *big*. And hard.

My own body reacted with another rush of slick heat, my nipples hardening into aching points. No longer caring to take things slow I pressed my body in against his and wrapped my hand around his heavy cock. He hissed as my palm connected with the silky skin, and again when I closed my mouth around one of his nipples and gave it a teasing flick with my tongue.

The heady scent of him hit my nostrils and filled my mouth. I wanted him so bad my body ached.

I wrapped my free hand around his back to caress the hard ropes of muscles there while I kissed and nipped my way down his torso, intent on my goal.

For every time my lips touched his skin or my hand

squeezed his pulsing cock he groaned softly, and the sound of it only spurred me on. I enjoyed the salty taste of his skin and the way he began to shake as my questing tongue neared its target. He may have been a rich and powerful alpha male, but right then, I was the one with all the power.

I dropped to my knees in front of him and took a moment to enjoy the view.

His cock was so thick I couldn't quite close my fingers around it, and long enough I'd be able to fit two hands along the shaft with ease. I briefly wondered if I'd even be able to take him in my mouth, but then decided there was only one way to find out.

When I swiped my tongue at the bloated, purple head, a full body shiver went through Marcus.

"Don't," he gasped.

I ignored him. The taste of his all-male musk ignited a shockwave of desire in my abdomen that spread down my thighs and made ripples of sharp need flood into my already tight clit. Groaning, I wrapped my lips around the tip of his cock and swirled my tongue to taste more of him. I just had time to be pleased with the discovery that yes, I could fit him in my mouth even if it would make my jaw ache within a minute, when a *growl* ripped from Marcus and his hands closed tightly around my arms.

I yelped when he roughly pulled me from my knees, lifting me up and swinging us both around until the kitchen island's smooth surface connected with my backside.

"What—?" My questioning gasp broke off midway through the sentence when he grabbed my arse in both hands, pulled me to the edge of the island, and buried his head between my thighs.

I jolted at the unexpected touch of his tongue diving in between my lower lips, and then groaned unintelligibly as shocks of pleasure followed.

He licked me with broad strokes, teasing at my entrance until my readiness flooded his tongue before he switched focus to my aching clit.

"*Ooh*, God," I moaned, slumping back on my elbows so I could arc my pelvis up against his talented tongue. Each flick of it against my tight bundle of nerves sent me higher and higher, and when he closed his lips around it and sucked, I couldn't hold back a sharp cry.

"I'm gonna come," I moaned in between breathless pants. "Oh, *fuck*, I'm going to—!"

Marcus gripped my thighs tighter so he could pull my pussy even closer, and I screamed. It only made him intensify his efforts tenfold. He suckled my clit so hard it was nearly too much, almost painful, but he held on to my thighs and arse so tight all my bucking and thrashing couldn't dislodge him.

I grasped wildly for his hair with both hands, but as my fingers wove into the black strands he let up on my poor clit for just a second, and I used my grip to yank him harder against me instead of pushing him away.

His next onslaught sent me flying over the edge, screaming like a woman possessed.

It took several minutes for the aftershocks to release my mind and body enough that I could let go of his hair, endorphins swathing my mind in the most ecstatic bliss I'd ever experienced.

"Wow," I mumbled groggily as I collapsed down on the counter, my overheated body relishing the cool marble.

When I found the will to open my eyes again, I saw Marcus standing between my thighs, leaning on the counter with both hands and breathing heavily as if he'd just run ten miles. The wildness in his eyes blazed, no longer restrained.

"Come here," I said, reaching a hand out for him.

He took it and pulled me upright, one arm snaking behind my body to haul me closer. The other he used to tip my chin up, but I was the one to stretch up and brush my lips against his.

My own flavor filled my mouth as he parted his lips and took me in, the hand on my chin moving around the back of my head to tangle in my hair.

I moaned into his mouth as he deepened our kiss, sparks of raw pleasure bursting through my well-prepared body.

"Take me," I gasped when he pulled back to let us both breathe. "I want to feel you inside me."

He growled low in his throat, hands constricting around my body for a moment before he pushed me back so he could kick off the remainders of his clothes. He stepped away, fisting his thick cock in one hand. Poised and ready to fill me.

The glorious sight made me shiver with anticipation, my pelvis lifting up in an involuntary invitation, but when he put his free hand on my thigh to open me up wider for his hips, I remembered something vital.

"Hang on," I croaked, reaching blindly behind me with one hand until it connected with my purse. I fumbled to get it open and quickly found what I was looking for.

"Condom," I said as I held out the little foil packet for him.

He stared at it for several breaths, and for a moment I thought he was going to refuse. Then he snatched it from me and slid the condom on with practiced ease, despite the obviousness of the tight fit, before returning his focus to me. He brushed both hands up along my inner thighs and then down again, spreading me open with his thumbs as if to test my readiness.

Not that there should be any reason to doubt if I was ready for him—I could *feel* my own slickness dripping from my entrance and pooling on the counter underneath me, and every cell in my body ached to be united with his.

"Please," I rasped.

Marcus fisted his cock again, pushing it gently against my already spread labia.

I groaned at the contact and lifted my hips to guide him in.

But despite my eagerness, Marcus went slow. He pressed against my entrance with agonizing care, letting my body adjust to being opened as his head drove slowly into my heat until *finally,* it popped in fully, seating itself just inside.

My whimper mingled with his sharp hiss. It was a tight fit, but his gradual entry made sure the sensation of being stretched wide was nothing but pleasurable.

*"More."*

He met my demand with more pressure, and I fell back on my elbows as he slowly drove in, spreading my channel all the way up until finally, his hips were completely flush with mine.

The rush of electricity that burst through me at finally being one with him was nearly as overwhelming as his heavy cock pulsing at the entrance to my womb, filling me up like nothing before it.

*"Evelyn."*

The guttural sound of my name made me look up into his eyes, and the swirl of emotion overwhelmed me. There was raw pleasure there, and the feral glint that had been present from the very beginning, but the fear and restraint was back now. He was fighting against the connection between us, I realized, but for the life of me I couldn't understand why.

Nothing had ever felt as good as his cock lodged to the hilt inside of me, my very core opening up wide to take everything he had to give. I didn't want him to hold back—I wanted him to lose himself with me.

"Don't fight it," I said, my voice hoarse but soft.

"I don't want to hurt you," he ground out, surprising me with the raw plea in his darkened gaze.

"You won't." I knew he had the capability to—his body was so big compared to mine, and that barely-contained ferocity in his eyes was impossible to ignore. But somehow, I knew he wouldn't. "Move with me."

Marcus moaned when I rolled my hips slowly against him and grabbed my waist. And then he moved.

I bit down on my lip until I tasted blood to stop myself from crying out, not wanting him to think he was hurting me, but *oh, sweet Jesus,* the feel of his overwhelming girth dragging against my inner walls was nearly more than I could bear.

His thrusts were slow but fully executed, and we gasped together each time he bottomed out in me. He hit every single delicious spot inside me, and it wasn't long before I wanted more, even though my body was still struggling with his size.

"God, yes, like that. Give me more. Please, I need more."

He responded by wrapping his arms around my torso

and lifting me up against him, capturing my mouth in a deep kiss as he rolled his hips up.

"*Mm-oh!*" I cried out, tipping my head back as gravity pulled me down on his cock just as he pushed up, reaching new depths in my unaccustomed pussy.

"*God!*"

It was too much, he filled me too deeply, but I didn't want it to stop. I wanted him to keep taking me until we were one, melted together by flesh and ecstasy. His next thrust was another slow, full roll of his hips, and I cried out and dug my nails deep into his shoulders.

A deep warning growl rumbled from Marcus' chest, but I was too lost in the sex to pay it much mind. When he drove into me again, I met him with a roll of my own hips, ripping his skin with my nails from the sheer intensity of taking him so deeply.

Marcus froze mid-movement, his arms locking tight around my body. I looked up, confused—and swallowed hard.

His eyes were blazing and so, so dark it looked like his pupils filled the irises completely. There was no restraint left, no fear. For the first time, I saw what Marcus Steel looked like when the beast inside him got unleashed, and it made every hair on my body stand on end.

"I—*omph!*" Before I managed to get so much of the beginning of an apology out, his lips crashed against mine, forcing them apart.

I moaned as his tongue lashed against my own, and

again when he pulled halfway out of my pussy—but when he drove back in, there was no trace left of his prior gentleness.

I tried to scream when he rammed into me with all the force his powerful body contained, but Marcus snuffed my voice with his savage kiss. When he pounded into me again I finally ripped my lips from his and threw my head back to give sound to the desperate cry clawing its way out of my throat. He didn't afford me any respite, fucking into me hard and fast. His lips and teeth found my neck, pressing bruising kisses to it while he ravaged me against the counter.

He was like a beast possessed, and I—I lost myself in him.

I came for him as I clung to his shoulders, the size of him forcing my pussy to submit with aching spasms that made my toes curl. I dug my nails into his skin as my climax rolled through my helpless body, prolonged by his continued pounding into me. He didn't stop, not even when I collapsed in a pile of melted bone and muscle on the counter in front of him. He simply shifted his grip to my hips so I could lay down on the marble while he kept pulling me onto his cock in hard thrusts.

I looked up at him from underneath hooded lids, too tired to begin another climb despite the delicious friction tantalizing the hypersensitive spots deep inside me. He was beautiful in his wildness, so strong and unbelievably male that it spoke to every primitive instinct within me.

His breath came out in harsh gasps and growls as he drove into me much harder than I should have wanted. Yet despite the pain—or maybe because of it—it felt so good I could hardly bear it.

My pussy tightened around his pounding girth, and I reached down to rub my clit. Sharp shocks of pleasure thrilled through my body and I mewled with want, canting my hips up for more, but before I could move he pulled out.

I frowned at the sudden sensation of being empty—incomplete—and opened my mouth to protest, but never got the chance. Marcus grabbed me by the hips and flipped me over, pulling my arse out and up before he plunged back into me.

"*Ooh!*" I cried out and arched up as high as I could go. He seized both my wrists in reply, trapping my arms behind my back as he pushed me down flat against the counter.

"You come for *me*," he growled against my nape, sending goosebumps down my spine. "Only me."

The next forty minutes were a blur of pleasure mixed with just the right kind of pain. As he'd demanded, I did come for him, multiple times, and when he finally joined me in climax I'd lost count.

His thrusts, rough and merciless for the entire session, became frantic, and he relinquished his hold on my arms to grab my hips and pull me onto him as hard as he could while I yelped and cried out with my own release.

My pussy spasmed around him, desperately clamping down on his meaty cock to stem the onslaught while wave after powerful wave of pleasure washed through me once more. But this time, it finally succeeded. Marcus froze behind me, groaning as his cock seized. Then he rocked gently a few more times before finally stilling, his hands coming down on the marble next to my face as he dragged in big gulps of air.

It took me a few minutes before I came down enough from my orgasm high to notice he was still inside of me, silent but shaking ever so slightly.

"That was incredible," I sighed, rubbing my sweaty face against his arm in a loving caress. Everything felt blissful, like I was floating, even though Marcus' softening cock had me solidly anchored. "Don't think I'll be walking for the next couple of hours, though. *Damn.*"

A moment's silence, and then...

"Did I hurt you?"

His voice sounded odd—almost broken.

I laughed, giddy after being fucked senseless and pumped full of endorphins, and planted a quick peck on his skin. " 'Course not. It was lovely. Ten-ten, would do again. Just not right *now*. Mind pulling out? I want to check if my legs still work."

He obeyed without hesitation, and I moaned softly at the sensation of being left empty and without the warmth of his body pressing against my backside. Gingerly, I straightened back up. Immediately my legs wobbled, and I grasped at the counter for support. Strong arms closed around me, and I squealed as I was hoisted up off the ground.

Marcus held me against his body, bridal style, and I relaxed in his embrace with a happy mewl. He smelled like sex and cologne, and the warmth of him made my already jellified body turn into a liquid puddle. I smiled up at him, and was caught off guard by the look in his eyes. There was so much wonder, as if looking at me was akin to watching the sun rise for the very first time, but also something else. Something that spoke of possession and other dark desires that made my heart thump faster in my chest.

Without a word he carried me into the bedroom and put me down in a luxurious pile of soft sheets and duvets before he curled up behind me.

I fell asleep shortly after, feeling safer and happier than I had in a very long time.

## FIVE

### EVELYN

It was still dark when I woke up with a start, heart pounding.

I blinked to regain my bearings, disoriented from being ripped out of the deepest sleep I'd managed in a long time.

A low whimper from my side pulled my attention.

"Marcus?" I whispered, squinting into the darkness in an attempt to see his face.

Another whimper, louder this time, made me fumble for the light on the nightstand next to me. Just as the soft light bloomed in Marcus' bedroom, another pained moan sounded from the bed.

I turned and found the large man curled into a fetal position, clutching the sheets in both hands. His face was drawn into a tight mask, but he was obviously still asleep.

"Marcus, you're having a bad dream," I called as I rolled all the way over to him.

He didn't respond, and I grabbed his shoulder and shook it gently. "Come on, baby. It's just a nightmare."

His lips parted and relief flooded me. *Thank God.* Seeing the powerful man so distraught filled me with unease.

But instead of waking, a soft wail escaped his throat. I'd never heard a sound like that from a human being, and it made my heart ache as if someone had closed a fist around it and squeezed. Whatever he was dreaming, it had to be bad. Really bad.

"*Marcus.*" This time, I put all my strength into shaking him, rolling him onto his back in the process. Not a small feat, considering his sheer size. "Wake up!"

His eyelids fluttered for a moment before finally, he opened them with a start. He stared up at me, a mixture of fear and confusion on his face.

"Shh, it's okay. You were having a nightmare," I said, curving my hand around his cheek in a soothing caress. Only when I touched his skin did I notice the wetness. He'd been crying.

Slowly, awareness slipped back across his features, and he frowned and lifted his hands to scrub them across his face, erasing the traces of his vulnerability.

"Sorry. Go back to sleep."

It was easy to see through his gruff tone—he had not meant for me to see him like this.

But I had. And even though I'd known Marcus for less than twelve hours, I couldn't bear the thought of him hurting.

"Do you want to talk about it?"

"No."

I rolled up over on one elbow and let my other hand rest against his chest. His heart was still beating much faster than it should. "Okay. It sounded like it was a really awful dream, though."

No answer.

I bit the inside of my cheek. It was no surprise that Marcus Steel had issues expressing his emotions. A man didn't develop the kind of terrifying presence he possessed by being all warm and open about what haunted him at night.

"Come here," I said, and when he lowered his hands to look at me, I lay back down and opened my arms.

To my surprise, he moved without objection, slipping into my embrace. The soft exhale of his breath as he rested his face on my shoulder blew across my right breast, raising the nipple.

His response was to stroke the underside of that breast and let a thumb graze the erect nipple up top. I shuddered in response, well-used muscles clenching weakly. I suppressed a wince. Yeah, I wasn't ready for *that* kind of comfort just yet.

Instead, I remembered how my mother used to comfort me when I'd had a bad dream, and stroking his naked back, I began humming. It was an old nursery rhyme, and for a moment I felt a bit silly soothing a grown man like this—but Marcus simply sighed, muscles relaxing and his hand on my breast stilling. So when the first melody was done, I started a new one, this time singing along.

I sang for what felt like the better part of half an hour until Marcus' breathing turned deep and steady, his body going limp against mine.

I looked down at the sleeping man in my arms as my voice died down. It wasn't until then that I realized I'd lost my fear for him somewhere between orgasms last night. Instead of someone inherently dangerous, I saw a man who'd locked away all his emotions until they exploded like they had when I'd accidentally hurt him. The darkness in him wasn't his—it was whatever he had locked up inside, whatever had made him withdraw into himself to the point he'd become completely unapproachable. Frightening in his solitude.

But beneath the surface, beneath the iron locks, I could sense the real Marcus Steel. And what lay underneath was a man I could see myself falling for all too easily. There had only been glimmers, but right from the start my body had recognized what my mind was finally coming to accept.

I wanted more of him than just one night. A lot more.

I stroked my fingers through his black strands,

relishing the pressure of his body against mine as I breathed in the scent of Marcus and our sex.

Too bad I was here on a job, and that if and when he found out, I better hope he never saw me again.

I had no idea what Marcus did for a living, but based on his luxurious flat and that he was in any way mixed up with Gerald Brigs, he was obviously very capable of inflicting pain if he needed to.

And the thief who seduced him to steal from him...? I had a distinct sense I'd fall into the category of "*needed to.*"

Suppressing the ache in my heart, I eased out from underneath Marcus' heavy body, doing my best not to wake him.

He groaned in protest when I slipped free, and I gave his face a quick glance to ensure he wasn't waking before I rolled all the way out of bed and let myself out of the bedroom.

I walked naked through the apartment to fetch my purse from the kitchen counter and then went hunting for wherever he kept his safe.

It didn't take me long. The first door I opened turned out to be his office, and on the wall nearest his desk a safe was built into the concrete. It wasn't even hidden behind a painting, as I'd somewhat expected it to be. Perhaps I watched too many detective shows.

I walked to the safe and tapped my nails against the black surface. It was a dial combination lock, and I had no idea what the hell the code could be. It wasn't like Marcus had mentioned any lucky numbers while we'd fucked.

Lost, I pulled the folded-up piece of paper Brigs had given me from my purse and sat on Marcus' leather office chair to study it.

It was mainly names, of family members I presumed, and only two numbers right next to each other. Dates, I realized, thirty-four years apart. I tried those first, with no luck.

*Come one, Evelyn. You can do this. What kind of numbers would a man like Marcus use to secure his belongings?* I chewed on a fingernail as I stared at the safe for a few minutes. There were no clues in the office—it was as devoid of personality and decorations as the rest of his flat... *Hang on.*

I let my gaze sweep over the list again, finding a familiar name again. Aidan. His nephew—and the only family member who had made it into a picture frame in Marcus' home. What was that date at the bottom of that frame?

I swiveled the chair back into position and half-jogged back to the living room, doing my best not to wince for each step. The reminder of what I'd spent the night doing was impossible to ignore. Guess that's what I got for breaking almost a year's worth of a dry spell with a stallion-sized ride rather than something a little more beginner-friendly.

The light from the city offered enough of a glow for

the quiet living room that I could easily navigate my way to the picture frame without turning on the lights. I picked it up, glancing at the cute baby before zeroing in on the date below the picture. The first of August 2015.

I hurried back to Marcus' office, doing my best to ignore the sense I was betraying someone much too good for me, and hunched over in front of the safe. Backing out now was going to do nothing but get me into some serious trouble with Brigs.

01-08-2015.

The clink of metal pins sliding into place from the safe's locking mechanism sent a little jolt through me and I bit the inside of my cheek as I pulled the heavy door open and looked inside.

There was a small pile of papers in the safe, a passport, and a couple of piles of fifty pound notes, along with a pen drive. I reached for the pen drive and quickly closed my hand around it, relieved that I'd managed the task I'd been set.

But just as I was about to close the safe, my eyes caught the piles of money again. There had to be nearly fifty thousand pounds in that safe.

Apart from tonight, I had never stolen in my life. Not even a pack of gum. My mother had raised me right. But of course, my mother couldn't have predicted I'd one day be under them thumb of mafia scum, paying back a loan I should never had accepted.

If I paid Brigs back in cash, I'd never have to work for him again.

The problem was, with my waitressing job, I would be in his debt for years to come. Maybe even a decade, the way he calculated interests. And here were stacks of money, right in front of me. If I took just £10,000 I could walk away from this job and never look back.

I bit my lip as my gut clenched. But I'd be stealing them. From Marcus. And not because I'd been forced to, but for my own personal gain. There was a difference of morality, even if it probably wouldn't technically be much worse than what I was already taking from him.

My hand hovered over one of the stacks of bills as I gnawed on the inside of my cheek with indecision—until a chilling thought struck me. If I completed this job successfully, there was nothing to stop Brigs from making me do it again to some other guy.

And I was pretty damn sure I wouldn't be as happy about climbing into bed with whoever else he pointed at.

I grabbed a stack of bills and quickly stuffed it into my purse next to the pen drive, zipped it close, and slammed the safe shut. Better a thief once than forced to steal and whore out my body indefinitely.

After making sure the office looked exactly like I'd found it, I snuck back to the living room where my clothes still lay in a pile on the floor, but as I bent for my underwear, I paused. If I left in the middle of the night, it would seem awfully suspicious. Much better if I stayed the night and left in the morning—it wasn't like he would think to check the safe while I was there, anyway.

I put my purse back on the counter where I'd left it the night before and tip-toed back to the bedroom, telling myself that my decision had nothing to do with wanting just a couple more hours of pretending like what I'd experienced in the arms of Marcus Steel had been real.

# SIX

## MARCUS

How could a human being be so completely and unabashedly perfect?

And so fucking beautiful? From the light sprinkle of freckles across her nose to her flaming hair and pink lips, Evelyn's face looked like it belonged to an angel. My own, personal angel whose voice alone made my nightmares melt away.

She sighed when I touched her cheek as gently as she touched mine last night in her attempt at comforting me.

I couldn't remember the last time anyone saw me in the aftermath of losing control like I did last night—I didn't know if anyone ever had, and the echo of her concern still rang inside of me, like a warm trickle from behind my ribs.

Was this what my brother felt for his wife? Was this

the woman who would have been mine, had things been different?

I pressed a hand to my chest when the pleasant sensation behind my ribs turned to a sharp ache and clenched my teeth against the rush of regret.

I lost control with her. I could have *hurt* her.

Though, when my conscience snapped into blackness from the sting of her nails, it didn't feel like it did all the other times. The split second I had to recognize what was happening, it wasn't a murderous rage that encapsulated my brain. It was... euphoric.

I closed my eyes for a moment, wishing with everything I was that there was a way this wouldn't be the last time I got to wake up with her in my arms.

I knew there was no point wishing for it, but I did it anyway. She was too pure, too innocent. Much as I wanted to give in to every roaring instinct in my body to claim her like some primitive beast, I couldn't. Someone so genuinely good shouldn't be tied to my darkness. But it felt good to pretend, even if only for a few seconds.

"Evelyn." Even the taste of her name on my tongue made me crave more of her.

"Mm?"

I opened my eyes at the sleepy grumble below me. Her eyes were open too now, if somewhat unfocused.

"Did you say something?"

Her sleep-roughened voice made me smile. She was so fucking cute. "Morning."

"Mmhm," she purred, and my body recognized the sultry undertone, immediately rendering me rock-hard. *God, how does she do that?*

I shifted, sliding the sheets down her naked body to move in between her legs, ready to fulfill the need I heard in her voice, but the sight of several finger-shaped bruises on her biceps and hips made me freeze, my heart dropping.

"I did hurt you."

"Hmm?" She followed my stare and shrugged when she spotted the marks on one hip. "Oh. It's fine."

It wasn't fine. It wasn't fine at all.

Disgusted with myself, I pulled back and got out of the bed before I got too lost in the need for another release between her thighs.

"No morning sex?" Evelyn said, and when I dared a glance at the bed, I caught her disappointed pout.

"No." Why was she so dead set on getting lost in my darkness? She knew what I was—I knew she saw what everyone sees when they meet me. Someone dangerous. Even the women who'd previously made it to my bed recognized it, but I knew they disregarded it for the draw of my body or power. I didn't understand why it wasn't like that with Evelyn, but I knew that wasn't why she told me to take her home with me. Almost like she felt the draw between us as keenly as I did, like she knew it was a bad idea but couldn't stop herself any more than I could.

"Breakfast?" I asked, because I needed to take my

mind off her dusky pink nipple peeking up above the sheets. I wanted to close my lips around it so bad.

"Nah, I need to leave soon anyway," she said with a sigh. "Thanks, though."

Hot, dark anger ripped at my insides, so unexpectedly I had to bite down on a pained grunt. *Leave?* She wanted to *leave* me?

It took me a couple of seconds to fight back the monster enough that I could muster a short nod. She was always going to leave, and it was for the best anyway. I had nothing to offer her—nothing but darkness.

Yes, she could have been my wife—in another life. But not this one.

"I'll take you home."

"Oh." Her voice betrayed her surprise. "No, that's not necessary."

I frowned at the dismissal. "Evelyn. I'm taking you home."

"No, you're not." Her tone changed abruptly, sharpness making its way into it for the first time since I met her. I could hear her get out of bed but resisted the urge to turn around and look at her. There was not enough willpower in the whole world to make me keep my hands off her if I saw her standing naked in front of me like she had last night.

"Evelyn—"

A quick kiss landed on my back, making a shiver

travel up along my spine before she waltzed past me and out of the bedroom.

I followed her mindlessly, trying and failing not to look at her round arse. She stopped next to the kitchen island and bent to pick up her clothes. I finally managed to turn away, before memories of what we did on that counter made me lose the final slivers of my already flagging self-control.

"I'm not letting you get a cab. I'll drive you."

"Stop trying to boss me around. You're not particularly scary with morning hair. Now shush and zip me up." She stepped around to my front, a mischievous smile on her face before she turned her back.

I zipped up her black dress, resisting the urge to let my fingers glide along her soft skin as I did.

"I'm a big girl. I can get home on my own," she said, turning around to look up at me. A flash of regret passed across her features, so quick I almost missed it, before she forced a smile on her face and raised up on her tiptoes to kiss my cheek. "Thank you for a wonderful night, Marcus."

I stared at her as she grabbed her bag, waved with her fingertips, and walked out my door. Leaving me.

The blinding pain as the monster bellowed its fury made me stumble forward, leaning heavily against the kitchen island.

*God, I need her. I need her. I...*

*...How did she know my name?*

---

IT HAD BEEN a long time since I felt so unsure of myself.

I'd been sitting in my car outside her run-down apartment block for nearly an hour, and it wasn't going to get me the answers I wanted. But the longer I stared at the door, the less sure I was of what would happen if I went in.

I gripped the steering wheel harder, doubt blooming in my chest as it had been since I'd grabbed my car keys and followed her taxi to her apartment.

She knew my name, and I was 100% sure I hadn't told her. I'd seen enough betrayal in this business to know never to ignore signs of things being off. But even as my innate mistrust gnawed at the back of my skull, I was still clutching the damn steering wheel.

Because if I was being honest, answers weren't what I was here for, not really. I was here because all I could think about was her arms wrapping around my neck and her lips pressing against mine.

I groaned and threw my head back against the headrest. *Fuck.* There had to be a logical explanation as to why she knew my name. If there was something wrong about her, I would have known. She was way too good, too pure to be mixed up in any business crap.

But what was a girl who lived in this shitty part of town doing at a club like *Eleonore?*

*Fuck!*

The truth was staring me in the face, even if I was too lovesick to want to acknowledge it.

Blackness flashed in warning from the sides of my vision and I pressed a hand to my chest to soothe the monster as I drew in deep breaths. When I finally got control of myself, I fumbled for my phone, my fingers tight. If she truly betrayed me, I wouldn't be able to push the darkness down—and despite the monster howling in my chest, I had enough control left to know what would happen if I snapped.

Flashes of her body lying in front of me, mutilated and bloody like the people I'd murdered in my past blackout rages, made me push "call" on the twins' phone number.

Thankfully, the line connected after only two rings.

*"Marcus? Is everything all right?"*

The concern in my brother's voice was understandable. I never called any of them unless it was an emergency.

And this—this was an emergency.

"You need to come. Both of you."

*"Okay. Can you give us an address, mate?"*

Right, an address—

Movement on the pavement next to my car caught my eye and I turned my head just in time to see a familiar figure walk past my Porsche and over to the the staircase leading up to Evelyn's flat.

Leo Brigs. The nephew of Gerald Brigs, the man my

brother Blaine threatened last year over a business deal gone wrong.

There was no longer any plausible deniability—if she was in with the Brigs, then she played me.

*"Marcus? Come on, mate, tell me where you are."*

I flicked my thumb across my phone's screen, hanging up. The monster growled low as I saw the door slowly close shut behind Leo.

# SEVEN

## EVELYN

When my front door finally slammed shut behind me, I let out a sigh of relief. I felt like the worst human being on the planet, and the only thing I needed was to be left alone with my own self-loathing.

I tossed my bag on my couch and stripped out of the black dress without stopping on my way to the shower. The sooner I could no longer smell Marcus on me, the sooner I could try to forget what I'd done.

Only the lukewarm spray from my semi-functioning shower couldn't remove the delicate ache between my legs, and with every step I took while I got dressed and poured myself a bowl of cereal, I was reminded of the man who had made me feel things I didn't even know existed.

If only things could have been different.

I sat down on my couch next to where I'd tossed my purse and put my breakfast down on the coffee table. The guilt in my gut made it difficult to eat.

Maybe if I saw what was on that stupid pen drive, I'd get some clarity?

With any luck, it would be a detailed description of how horrible a person Marcus really was. Perhaps then I could hand it over to Brigs without feeling like I'd betrayed someone who didn't deserve it.

I got the pen drive out of my purse and plugged it in my laptop. As I waited for the machine to fire up, I contemplated the wad of cash I'd stolen from Marcus. Perhaps I should just throw away whatever was on that drive and tell Brigs I hadn't been able to get the combination to Marcus' safe, and then promptly pay them the money I owed them so they wouldn't have time to get too pissed. That way I might still have stolen from Marcus, but at least I wouldn't betray him. I didn't know what his relationship was to the Brigses, but if they had someone try to steal information from him, I assumed they were not his friends.

Yeah, that seemed like a good backup plan, in case whatever was on the pen drive didn't show Marcus murdering baby animals for sport.

When my ancient laptop finally managed to boot up, I quickly navigated to the pen drive's folder. There was only a single file on there—a video.

*Great.* And what sort of video would a crime lord like

Gerald Brigs be interested in? I clicked it, hoping against hope that I wasn't about to watch something that would haunt me for the rest of my life.

The image that flickered into view was a little off-kilter, but clear enough. It seemed to have been shot inside a stately lounge or living room with thick carpets and mahogany furniture, but from a weirdly high angle. It looked like someone had planted a camera on the ceiling. A surveillance camera, perhaps?

I jolted when I spotted movement on the video. An older, but handsome man with steel-gray hair and cold, gray eyes came into focus. He was pacing back and forth across the thick carpet, arms folded across his chest and his mouth pulled into a narrow line.

*"You know there's only one thing to do."* The man's voice was a bit distorted from the audio, but the words themselves were clear enough. I couldn't see who he was talking to, but the way he was staring across the room while he spoke it was obvious he wasn't alone.

*"He always was so goddamn cocky. I should have known that kid would be trouble. And now he thinks he can usurp me? His own father?!"*

Whoever he was talking to responded, but the audio wasn't clear enough for me to make out the words. The man in the frame shook his head, the angry slant to his mouth only becoming more pronounced. *"If I give him a second chance, he'll just see it as a weakness and pounce. I raised my boys well. Too bad Jeremy didn't listen when*

*I taught them the Steel motto: 'Everything for family.' Well, if he thinks he can bite the hand that feeds him, it's time to cut him loose. I want him dead before the week is over."*

My stomach dropped as my brain caught up to the silver-haired man's words. The *Steel* motto...? This was... was this Marcus' *dad?*

And this Jeremy he wanted killed... was that Marcus' brother?

Oh, my God. The pen drive contained proof that Marcus' father wanted to kill his brother. Had he succeeded? Marcus had only mentioned his brother, Blaine, but then again—tragic family loss probably wasn't what most people talked to their one-night stands about.

But why was he hiding this video? For blackmail? Insurance? Proof?

Why did Brigs want it?

I frowned. The man was giving instructions as to how the person off-camera should go about murdering his son. He seemed calm and cool through the entire exchange, if a bit annoyed. As if having to plan out his own son's murder was a major inconvenience to his busy schedule.

The video cut off shortly after, static filling the screen.

I sat back on my sofa, numb. I don't know what I'd imagined I would find, but it certainly wasn't that. I'd expected something money-related, not... intimate family issues that stretched way beyond your standard petty feuds. I recalled my mum not speaking to an aunt when I was a kid, all because someone hadn't given back a sugar bowl they'd borrowed. This was something else entirely.

"Well, well, our little honey trap caught a nice, fat fly!"

I squealed at the unexpected voice from behind me, adrenaline spurring me off the couch and onto my feet. I spun around, only to come face to face with Leo Brigs.

I gaped, staring at the wide-set man as he looked over my shoulder at the screen. "What are you doing in my flat? Get out!"

"I came to see if you were still alive, sugar tits. Didn't entirely expect you to pull one over on that big brute, but look at you proving me wrong! Seems uncle was right when he said you'd be perfect for the job. I'd have picked one of our high-class hookers, myself, but Marcus is into chunky girls, huh? Did he give it to you good?"

He leered at me, and my shock gave way to disgust.

"I want you to leave," I hissed, folding my arms across my chest and wishing I'd put a bra on underneath my t-shirt.

"Sure. Just give me the pen drive. Though once we've had a look at it, I'll be back for details on your night with the Steel freak. For research, of course. Maybe we can reenact parts, eh?"

I looked from his outstretched hand to his filthy smirk, and something snapped in me. The thought of this creep watching the video of Marcus' father betraying his family made my stomach clench. I didn't know why the Brigs wanted it, but I knew they'd use it against him somehow. And as I looked at Leo, standing there so self-assured in my living room, as if he had every right to be there even though I hadn't invited him in, I knew I couldn't let that happen.

Without further thought, I bent and pulled the pen drive out of its socket, snapping it clean in two.

"What the fuck did you just do?" Leo's smug voice morphed into a furious roar. "What the *fuck*, bitch!"

I had time to feel maybe two seconds' worth of triumph before Leo's right hand closed painfully around my wrist as he yanked me forward, putting his face an inch from mine. The rage distorting his features made me swallow hard, a fresh rush of fear flushing away any hint of triumph.

"You are going to regret that, you stupid little cunt."

---

THE HOUSING BLOCK Leo took me to wasn't the usual place I had my meetings with the Brigses.

It was in one of the absolute worst parts of town, with most of the windows in the red brick, rundown buildings around the filthy street either broken or boarded up. A few junkies sat against the wall next to the door leading into the building, but they were so far gone they didn't even look up when Leo dragged me across the asphalt by my arm, heedless that I was stepping in broken glass and dirt with my bare feet.

Inside, complete darkness met us until Leo hit his hand against the wall, triggering a worn light switch. A dim, naked bulb spread a sickly orange light, revealing a narrow corridor and a flight of stairs. It reeked of vomit and feces, and smears of a questionable nature covered the walls.

Leo continued down the hallway, never releasing his painful grip on my arm, and when we turned a corner and were faced with a flight of metal stairs leading to the basement level, he pulled me down them so fast I nearly tripped. Only his hold on me kept me upright.

Another hallway marked with brown patches led past several closed doors with peeling paint. By the seventh, Leo stopped and turned the knob, opening it.

I swallowed thickly at the sight inside—a single chair bolted to the floor with leather straps attached. And underneath it was a grate. A power hose hung on the far well, and by the door was a small desk with an old office chair. The scene was lit with a naked light bulb only slightly less orange than the ones lighting our path here.

I hadn't bothered pleading with Leo since he dragged me from my home. I knew enough about how they operated to know that no amount of begging would help me. It wasn't something I'd thought about when I'd broken the pen drive—it had been a purely instinctual reaction caused by an overpowering urge not to let this man and his uncle hurt Marcus.

Hopefully the money would help. I glanced at my purse that swung from Leo's grip. He'd grabbed it when he searched it for a copy of the pen drive and found the cash instead. I just hoped Gerald would make an appearance before his nephew hurt me so bad I wouldn't be able to walk away from it. While Gerald was cold and cunning and unlikely to grant any leniency for my actions, he was also a businessman. Money was the only thing I'd ever seen change his mind.

Inside the room Leo pushed me into the chair and pointed at me with a finger as if it was a knife. "Don't even think about running, bitch, or I'm cutting off your toes."

I didn't reply, but found it wisest to do as he said. I'd seen what he was capable of.

We waited in silence for what felt like an eternity before footsteps rang from the corridor behind the closed door. Moments later the handle turned, and Gerald stepped in flanked by two of his usual goons.

The elderly man looked severely out of place in the dank basement, his woolen coat and fedora sticking out against the marred walls like a sore thumb.

His cool eyes slid over me in the chair and then to his nephew. "What's this then, Leo? Your text said Evelyn is working for the Steels?"

"That's a lie," I said, glaring at Leo. "I've never met any of them until last night."

Gerald turned his attention back to me. "Oh? And did things not go according to plan, my dear?"

"They did, but I..."

"She watched what was on the drive and broke it so we wouldn't see," Leo seethed. "That fucking cunt! Months! It took us months to track that lead!"

Gerald's eyebrows inched up half an inch. "You broke it? Now, why would you do something that silly, Evelyn? What could possibly have been on that video that would make you take such a silly, silly risk?"

I bit my lip, my brain working overtime to try to come up with an answer that would help me out of this situation. It came up blank.

"I... there was nothing on it, really. Just... it was a sex tape. Of Marcus. I didn't... I didn't want you to see it. He's a nice guy, it would be humiliating."

Gerald narrowed his eyes ever so slightly at me. "You're making the mistake of lying to me, girl. I wouldn't advice you repeat that. Now, I'm going to ask you nicely one last time—what's on that video?"

"Please, I can pay you. I know I messed up, but I... I have ten grand in my purse," I nodded toward my bag Leo had tossed on the desk. "Take it."

"Probably money Steel paid to make her fuck us over," Leo growled from the desk.

"It's not. It was in the safety box with the pen drive. I stole it."

Gerald sighed sadly, but his eyes remained cool.

"What was on that video is much, much more valuable than ten thousand dollars. It's a pity—you had such a sweet face. I don't know of anyone else who could have seduced Marcus Steel. But... all good things must come to an end. Leo—make sure she tells you everything that was on that video. And when you're done, make sure no one will find her body."

# EIGHT

EVELYN

I told Leo what was on the video.

And then I told him everything else he asked, in between sobbing and begging for the pain to stop. And while I did, I hated myself for having been so stupid to throw my own life away because I wanted to protect a man I'd known less than twenty-four-hours.

"Please, stop! I'm sorry!"

"You're sorry? Guess you should have thought about that before you switched sides. How did he make you do it? Was it money, or did he just stuff your snatch that well?" Leo pulled back the hand he'd been punching repeatedly into my stomach, looking over his knuckles as if to see if he'd caused himself any damage.

"He didn't do anything," I gasped between dry heaves. "I f-felt guilty. He was so kind to me, a-and I b-betrayed him."

Leo snorted. "*Kind?* Marcus Steel? Did he go down on you or somethin'?"

"Yes." I was beyond trying to make the savage brute in front of me understand complex emotions I hardly grasped myself, and if confessing to the physical details of what had happened between Marcus and I would stop the torture, then I was willing to surrender any scraps of pride I had left.

Leo's eyes gleamed as he gave me a lecherous smirk. "Yeah? He lick you real good? Did you return the favor?"

"No. H-he didn't want me to."

"That's a real shame. I reckon ol' Marcus would have benefited from a good blowjob. Get some of the crazy sucked right out of his dick." He grabbed me by the jaw and forced my head back, smiling down at me. "Let's see if you can show me just how good you would have sucked his cock, hmm?"

Despite everything he'd put me through so far, I paled when I realized what he wanted and my stomach lurched. "No!"

The sting of his hand against my cheek shut me up, tears prickling my eyes. In front of me Leo fumbled with his pants, undoing his zipper and pulling out his semi-erect cock.

Panic tore at my insides as I struggled against the ropes he'd tied me to the chair with. *No. No, no, no!*

Leo fisted his cock and pointed at me with his free

hand. "Now, you be a good little girl and suck, and the rest of our time together is going to be a lot less painful for you. But if you bite, I'm pulling out every last one of your teeth, you got it?"

I didn't reply, couldn't, as panicked sobs tore up through my throat. I struggled uselessly in my bindings, wishing desperately for a miracle—anything to save me from getting raped. I don't know why the thought of Leo forcing me to pleasure him was even worse than the torture, but it was, and when he grabbed my jaw again and forced my mouth open, I wished for death.

A loud *boom,* followed by the unmistakable sound of splintering wood, echoed through the basement. Leo pulled back with a startled curse and spun around. I gaped up at the hulking figure who stood on top of the broken remains of the door.

Marcus.

An unmistakably pissed off Marcus, eyes as black as tar and pure hatred vibrating off every fiber of his being.

I didn't have time to wonder how the hell he was here before he stalked over to Leo and grabbed him around the neck with one large hand, his knuckles bulging as he squeezed.

Leo gargled and swung at his attacker, but the blows seemed to have zero effect on Marcus. Growling like an animal, he lifted the other man up by his throat and, when Leo's hand impacted with his head, Marcus grabbed it and *pulled.* The sickening sound of bones breaking and flesh tearing made me scream loud and shrilly, but neither of the two men paid me any mind.

Leo gargled brokenly in Marcus' grip, his eyes bulging as his face turned blue, but it was the pulsing blood from where his hand should have been that made me vomit violently onto the floor.

With a snarl Marcus threw him on the floor like a rag, and then he pounced.

He was vicious with his kill, like a beast descending on its prey. Blood splattered across the room as he ripped and shredded, his muscles bulging with the effort. At one point he tore so savagely that the backward jerk sent his arm into my chair, breaking it underneath me.

I fell to the floor with a cry, but Marcus was too consumed with the gore to even notice.

The only mercy was that as the chair broke, my right wrist and left ankle slipped free of their bindings. I scrambled on the floor to get away from the butchering happening by my side and managed to crawl to the wall, where I clawed at the ropes still shackling my left wrist and right ankle until finally, I was free.

Carefully, I got to my feet using the wall for support, gasping from the pain in my body and feet.

"Marcus." I don't know why I called out to the man still beating at the bloody, mauled corpse that had once been Leo Brigs. Perhaps because, despite the horror in front of me, and despite my terror at seeing someone killed so ruthlessly, I knew he had saved my life. Or perhaps some stupid part of my heart still clung on to the emotions he had awoken in me last night.

The large man froze, his muscles trembling as a shudder rolled through his powerful body. Slowly, he turned his head to look at me over his shoulder, as if some part of him recognized my voice or the sound of his name.

I gasped, unable to stop myself from cringing back against the wall.

The darkness in his eyes was much the same as when he'd snapped while we had sex—all consuming, blotting out every trace of the man I knew lived behind it. But this time, there was a difference. This time, it was not lust or need flaming behind his gaze—it was a fury so deep it extinguished everything he was, leaving nothing but a raging monster in its wake.

He looked at me for three long seconds, neither of us moving. Then, with a low growl, he turned back to the corpse on the floor and dug his fingers into the bloody flesh.

My breath exploded out in a shaky gasp. Whatever he was right now, he wasn't the Marcus I'd met. He wasn't the same man who had cried in my arms and made love to me like I was the only woman in the world.

Despite my trembling, I managed to make my feet move. As quietly as I could, I crept over to the desk and snatched my purse. And then I ran.

I DIDN'T WANT to go back to my flat, but I knew I had to. I needed to change clothes to something without blood smears, and I needed socks and shoes as well as my passport. I didn't stop to pack any clothes, nor to take care of my badly cut and bleeding feet. I knew I had no time.

I needed to be out of the city before nightfall, or I was dead. It didn't really matter if Gerald Brigs or Marcus found me first; there was no way I would survive another encounter with either of them, so I did the one thing I could—I prepared to flee the country.

But there was one stop I had to make before I left England for good: the nursing home where my mother lived. I had to tell my mum goodbye. Even if she wouldn't remember, I had to see her one last time.

My heart gave an achy spasm as I stuffed my passport into my purse with the cash I'd stolen from Marcus, and I wiped the beginnings of my tears away and closed the door to my flat behind me. There wasn't time to grieve yet —there wasn't even time to process all the horrible things that had happened since Leo broke into my home. Right now, I had to focus on survival, or I wouldn't see another sunrise.

I hailed a cab from the street and told him the address of my mother's nursing home as I climbed in the back. The driver sent me a mildly concerned look through his rear-view mirror, probably because of the big bruise blooming across my eye where Leo struck me. I looked out the window and pretended like I didn't see him, and after a second or two he set the cab in motion and pulled into the busy London traffic.

The nursing home where my mother lived was as quiet as always when I entered through the sliding doors.

"Evelyn, you're here early this week," Susie, the receptionist, said in greeting. Her smile faded when she caught a look at my face. "Is everything all right?"

I touched a hand lightly to my eye, wondering if I should have taken the time to try and cover it up. "Yeah, just... an accident. How's my mum?"

The woman's gaze lingered on my face for a moment longer before she seemed to dismiss it. "The nurses said she's having a difficult day. But I'm sure she'll be happy to see you."

I nodded and gave her a polite smile before I headed down the hallway to my mum's room. I had hoped she was having a good day today, so maybe she would be able to remember my visit during her lucid moments, but there was no time to wait. I just had to hope that somehow she would know that I hadn't abandoned her.

My mother sat in the chair by the window, her hair fanned out around her shoulders like a white sheet as she watched the birds in the tree outside. I had paid extra to make sure she got a room with a bit of a view—she'd always been so fond of her garden. Some of my happiest memories involved our many long hours tending to her veggie patch.

"Hi, Mum," I called as I closed the door behind me.

She turned from the window at the sound of my voice, her brows pulling into a frown. "What are you doing in my house? Are you an intruder?"

I ignored the stab of pain in my heart that always happened on the days she couldn't remember who I was.

"No, Mum, it's me—Evelyn. Your daughter." I walked over and sat on the chair opposite her, knowing from experience the coffee table between us was enough distance that I wouldn't scare her. "I've come to visit."

"I don't have a daughter," she said, staring at me as if I was trying to determine if I was an impostor. Then her expression softened a bit. "But... you do look like my sister, Agatha. She has such beautiful red hair, just like you. I... it's so hard to remember these days. Maybe we should call her?"

I reached out and took her hand in mine. It was as soft and warm as I remembered all through my childhood, even though it was so frail in my light grip now. "Yeah, maybe we can do that in a bit. I really just wanted to see you and chat for a while. I miss you."

"Oh. Okay." A glimmer of what she'd been seemed to light up behind her pale green gaze, and she gave my hand on top of hers a pat. "Let's chat a bit, dear."

I talked to her about nothing at all, just basking in her

presence and kind smile and the warmth of her hand in mine. We looked at the birds outside the window and laughed at two squirrels chasing each other up the tree trunk until the sky began to darken and I noticed Mum's focus started to slip.

With a start I realized I'd been there for a few hours, and it was well past time I left if I wanted a chance to get out of London without risking another run-in with the city's violent underworld.

"Mum, I have to go now," I said, doing my best to suppress the lump in my throat when I looked at her for what I knew would be the last time. Physically, she had aged with grace, and despite her white hair and lacking memory, she was still the same woman who had raised me on her own and given me everything she could. She was the only person I had left in the world—and I had to leave her.

"And I'm not going to be able to come around much anymore. I have to go away for a while."

She frowned at me. "You're going?"

"Yes. I don't want you to worry, okay? I'm going to be all right." With another glance at the dusky sky, I got up. Every part of my heart cried out to stay just a little bit longer, but I knew I had to go. I leaned over the table and gave her cheek a kiss, inhaling the scent of my mother one last time. Lavender and soap and something distinctly *Mum*. I wanted to remember it forever.

"Goodbye, Mum." I bit the inside of my cheek so hard

I tasted blood just to hold back the tears blurring my vision as I turned and made my way to the door.

"Wait," she called behind me.

My heart jolted and I turned back, a small ray of relief making its way through my depression. All I wanted was to say goodbye to her while she remembered who I was.

"Agatha? Is that you?" Her lips spread in a surprised and delighted smile.

I smiled back and blew her a kiss before I walked out the door and closed it behind me.

It took a couple of minutes before I'd pulled myself together enough to walk away from my mum's room and back down to the reception area.

Susie looked up when I rounded the corner, offering me a comforting smile. I took it my face reflected exactly how I felt.

"She'll have a good day the next time you come visit, or the time after that."

I nodded and swallowed the stubborn lump in my throat. "Susie, I... I have to go away for a while, and I don't know for how long but I think it might be... a very long time. I won't be able to stop by to check on my mum. Will you please check in on her once in awhile? Just sit down and watch the birds with her? She likes that."

"Love, what's going on?" Susie frowned at me, her eyes darting to my bruise again. "Are you in some kind of trouble? Do you need me to call someone? The police?"

"No, I'm... I'm fine. I just can't come by anymore.

Please, Susie. Please promise me you'll look after her?" I fumbled in my purse and pulled out five thousand pounds from the stolen stack of fifties. "I'll send more, for her stay. I just need to know that she'll be looked after. She..." I bit my lip, stopping myself before I broke down in tears.

Susie slowly closed her hands around the money, and though her face was still drawn in a worried frown, she nodded. "You know I'll look after her, Evelyn. But what do you want me to tell her, if she asks for you?"

I shook my head and looked down, breathing in through my nose to calm myself. "Just that I love her, and I'll be back as soon as I can. And..." I steeled myself to look into the other woman's eyes, willing her to understand the importance of the next bit. "And if anyone should come asking for me, tell them you've never heard my name before. It's safest that way."

Susie paled a bit, but nodded again. "Okay, Evelyn. Be safe."

I gave her a weak smile, unwilling to make a promise I wasn't sure I could keep. "Thank you."

I had thought the first time I walked into the nursing home when my mother moved in was a tough day, but it was nothing in comparison to today—to leaving for the last time. It took everything I had not to lose my mind as I walked out through the sliding doors.

The dark street outside was nearly empty, and I hurried along the pavement to get to the nearest station where I knew there'd be more people and I wouldn't be alone. I tried my best to push down my anxiety as I turned down the small road that connected to the station a few blocks down.

I only made it maybe twenty yards before someone grabbed me from behind, pressing a cloth into my mouth and a bag over my head.

# NINE

EVELYN

I squinted at the sudden light when the bag was pulled off my head.

I didn't know where I was or who had taken me, and my heart hammered a terrified beat behind my ribs. Whoever it was, I knew this wasn't going to end well for me.

After they snatched me, I'd been thrown in the back-seat of a car with my hands zip-tied behind my back. My abductor had driven for perhaps half an hour or more before he stopped and slung me over his shoulder, carrying me to this room and sat me down in a chair. There had been stairs, and I had a sickening feeling that I was back in the horrible basement where I had thought I would die. Well, perhaps that premonition would still come true.

But once my my pupils got accustomed to the light, I

noticed it was brighter and less orange than that basement had been, and there were no stains on the walls. The stench of blood and human decay was also absent.

I had an odd moment of relief, as if my upgraded cell meant that perhaps things weren't as bad as I'd thought—until I finally spotted my captor.

Marcus stood in front of me, arms folded across his wide chest and his handsome face drawn into dark, angry lines.

"*Mmph!*" My panicked cry was muffled by the cloth in my mouth as I jolted backward in my seat in an attempt to get away from him. Flashes of the blood spraying around him as he descended on Leo like a feral beast flashed in my mind's eye, and any relief I may have felt vanished in a rush of panic-fueled adrenaline.

"We need to talk," he said, his voice as grim as his face. Unfazed by my flinch when he reached out toward me, he pulled the cloth from my mouth and tossed it on the floor. "I suggest you cooperate."

I nodded shakily without taking my eyes off of him. Though he was clearly very, *very* angry, the ferocity I'd seen in his gaze the moment our eyes locked in Brigs' basement wasn't there now, and whatever else might happen, I knew my best chance of survival was to not provoke it to reappear.

"What did Brigs want from me?"

"A-a pen drive," I whispered.

His eyes widened for a moment and then narrowed to slits. "Did you get it?"

I nodded again.

Marcus' lips flattened for a moment. "How?"

The shame that filled me surprised me. He had me tied up and at his mercy, and was possibly going to kill me before the night was through—and I still felt *guilty* for what I'd done? Clearly, something was very wrong with me.

"Your nephew's birthdate. You—it was obvious he means a lot to you, and I figured..."

His eyes glowed with fury at my revelation, and I shrank back in the chair, terrified he'd lose control again.

"Did you steal anything else?"

"Money," I confessed, the shame returning with force. "T-ten thousand pounds. B-but I have five of them in my purse, you c-can have them back."

Marcus arched an eyebrow at me. "Brigs told you to steal money from me, along with the pen drive?"

"No, I... I needed it. And I'd already stolen the pen drive, so..." My attempt at an explanation died under his stare.

He rolled his shoulders as if to work out his anger and began to pace in front of me. I was somewhat relieved that I no longer had his burning eyes glued to my face and slumped back in the chair. I was more exhausted than I'd ever been in my life.

"How long have you been in Brigs' employ?"

"A year and a half." Had it really been that long? A year and a half of fear and self-hatred.

"A faithful employee," he gritted out, and I shrank back under another of his glares. "And certainly very valuable, if you could fool me like you did. Why did they harm you?"

"I broke the pen drive," I whispered, no longer able to meet his gaze. I lowered it to my feet. One of my shoes had come off while I struggled against him as he carried me to his car, but at least my ankles weren't tied up this time.

"You *broke* it?"

"I... after we... I wanted to know why Brigs wanted it so bad. If he was going to hurt you somehow. So I... I watched it, and I... couldn't make myself do it. I couldn't give it to him after I saw... So I broke it."

"You saw the video?"

"Yes." Too late I realized that admitting to being the only person to see what was on the pen drive was the stupidest thing I could have done. Looking back up, I backtracked, "But I didn't tell Gerald what was on it, that's why Leo tortured me. Please, Marcus, don't hurt me. Y-you don't have anything to fear from me, I promise. I'll leave London, Brigs won't find me. I won't tell a soul."

If he was affected by my frantic begging, his expression didn't betray it. He simply stared at me in silence for a few long moments, his face still twisted in anger. Then, without a word, he turned around and left the room.

What now? I sank back into the chair, spent and terrified.

Marcus came back through the door about ten minutes later, but the sight of the tub of steaming water in his hands and the towel over his shoulder didn't exactly provide me with any more clues as to his plans for me. When he pulled a knife and cut my wrists free before he knelt down in front of me, placing the tub by his side, my confusion was complete.

"W-what are you doing?"

He didn't answer me, and I flinched when he grabbed my shoe-free ankle in one hand. But he was strong and held on, and I didn't dare fight him.

Once I stopped moving, he carefully peeled off my sock and tossed it next to me, and I saw patches of blood on it. I peered down at my now bare foot and grimaced. It was filthy, and judging by the throbbing pain in my soles, I could hazard a guess how badly cut it was.

Marcus continued to my other foot, pulling both the shoe and equally blood-stained sock off it.

At the sight of their condition he made a dismayed sound deep in his throat and then proceeded to pull the tub in front of me so he could dip both my feet in the water.

"*Ow*," I whimpered when the heat closed around my wounds. I tried to pull my feet back, but Marcus held on. He looked like he wasn't even remotely straining to keep me still.

"What are you doing? It hurts!"

"It's saltwater," he said, not bothering to look up from the tub. "You'll get an infection."

I blinked, stunned when it finally dawned on me what he was doing. He was... cleaning my wounds? Slowly, I stopped struggling as the initial pain faded and just watched the large man who had hunkered down in front of me to care for my cut feet.

Did this mean he wasn't going to hurt me? I couldn't imagine anyone in the mafia world caring for the wounds of someone they were going to murder anyway, and the first tendrils of relief flooded me.

Once he seemed satisfied that I wasn't going to try and escape the foot bath, Marcus let go of my right foot and grabbed the left one, easily lifting it up to balance on his knee so he could inspect the sole. He dug a hand into one pocket and produced a couple of bandages, a small metal pot, and a pair of tweezers. Then, with a firm grip on my ankle, he began plucking small shards of glass from my damaged foot.

I winced and whimpered all the way through, and had to steel myself to not kick him when he pulled at some of the deeper splinters, but the salve he rubbed on after was soothing and his fingers impossibly gentle while he covered the wounds with a bandage.

After he was done with my second foot, he wiped his salve-covered hands in his pants and finally looked back up at me.

"Thank you," I said softly. "You didn't have to do that."

He didn't respond, his face still disturbingly grim—an expression that completely contradicted the gentleness with which he'd tended to my damaged feet.

But despite his persistent anger with me, the fact that he had taken care of my wounds made something inside of me click into place. I might have seen him brutally slaughter another human being, but as I looked down at him from my perch on the chair, I knew he wouldn't hurt me.

"I'm sorry," I said. "I didn't want to lie to you, or steal. Brigs... I owe him a lot of money, so I..."

"You're a honey trap," he said calmly, though his expression never changed.

"Yeah."

"You've done this before."

I opened my mouth to protest, but I doubted he cared about the differences between what I'd done in the past and what I'd done to him. "I didn't want to do it to you too," I said softly. "I know you probably don't believe me, but... if I hadn't, Brigs would have hurt me."

"He hurt you anyway," he said, letting his eyes linger on my swollen eye.

"Is that why you killed him?" I don't know what made me brave enough to ask, but the words tumbled out of my mouth before I could reconsider.

Marcus looked at me for a long moment, but he didn't

reply. Instead he said, "You put yourself in harm's way to protect me and my family. I am grateful. But I can't let you leave. I hope you understand that."

I gaped at him, caught between shock that he said he was *grateful* to me and worry over what he meant by not being able to let me leave. "Why not?"

"You saw what was on the video. I can't risk Brigs or anyone else catching you again," Marcus said as he got up from his kneeling position. He began to pace back and forth in the small cell like a lion in a cage.

"I promise, I won't ever use it against you. I won't tell anyone. Just let me leave, please," I begged him. "I won't ever return to England."

"Perhaps you are telling the truth. Perhaps not. But that doesn't make the threat to my family any less. Brigs could find you. Or someone else could. We have many enemies and no room to take chances."

"What if..." I looked up, an odd bolt of hope spreading in my stomach. It was an insane idea—he was a *killer*, and he had every reason not to want anything more to do with me, but... "What if we made a deal? You protect me from Brigs, and in return I stay with you."

He stopped his pacing, arching an eyebrow at me, and I grimaced.

"Not here, not like a prisoner. In your flat. I'll... be your companion. I'll make your food, do your laundry... share your bed."

His brows furrowed as he stared me down, and some of my enthusiasm withered under his gray gaze.

"Okay," he said after what felt like several long minutes, surprising me.

"Yeah?" I asked, relief slowly starting to seep through my battered body. It might technically be prostitution, but it didn't feel like it. Not with him.

"On one condition," he continued, leveling me with an inscrutable stare. "You agree to have my child."

# TEN

EVELYN

"Your *child?*" I repeated, not entirely sure I'd heard him right. "I... what? *Why?*"

"I want a family," he said without a hint of emotion in his voice, as if that was all the explanation needed.

I gaped up at him, too stunned to even argue the insanity in his premise. If he thought I was going to agree to this, he was nuts. Sure, I was inexplicably happy enough to spend the foreseeable future as his pretend-girl-friend until Brigs was no longer a threat to either of us, but a *baby?* Nuh-uh. Not going to happen.

But... I could always pretend like I agreed. I was on birth control, after all. All I'd need was to find an excuse to get him to take me by my flat and I'd have three months' supply of baby-nixing pills at my disposal.

And what was the alternative? Spend the next few weeks in this cell?

"Okay," I said, my voice a bit shaky even though I knew I wasn't planning on following through with this part of our deal. Saying the words out loud still felt scary. "Okay, I'll have your baby."

---

THE CAR RIDE TO MARCUS' flat passed in silence, like it had the last time we took this journey together. Only this time, the electric silence in the car wasn't so much sexual tension as it was... I didn't even know what the hell it was. I glanced at Marcus by my side, whose focus was purely on the road ahead of us. The moment I'd agreed to his crazy arrangement, it was as if a switch flipped behind his dark gaze and most of the resentment disappeared. He had even carried me to the car so I wouldn't have to walk on my bandaged feet.

For all intents and purposes, Marcus seemed to be completely over my betrayal and everything that had followed.

I wasn't anywhere near over any of the things that had happened in the past day, but as I sat with my head leaned against the car window and watched the darkened city rush past us, I felt inexplicably calm. Whatever else Marcus was, there was not a bone in my body that didn't believe he could keep me safe from Brigs. He might be a thousand times more terrifying than Gerald Brigs, but in the depths of my soul I knew he wasn't going to unleash the terrifying darkness he carried around on me. In fact, sitting next to him as we drove through the dark streets made me feel more safe than I had in a very long time.

I frowned into the darkness. I'd seen him literally shred another human being, seen the all-consuming rage in his eyes where no shred of humanity remained. Not to mention, he basically wanted to use me as a broodmare— not something a sane guy would suggest. But still... it felt better than I could put into words knowing that no one would hurt me ever again, as long as Marcus was around.

When he pulled into the parking basement underneath the fancy high-rise his penthouse was located in some twenty minutes later, I had given up trying to sort through any of the day's events. I was too exhausted, both physically and emotionally, to even begin processing everything, and when Marcus walked around to the passenger side and picked me up as if I was no heavier than a child, I simply rested my head against his arm and let him carry me to the elevator.

He didn't put me down until we were inside his flat, easily disposing of me on the kitchen island before he shrugged out of his woolen coat and headed over to look into the fridge.

I looked around the familiar space and let my hands slide over the countertop. It seemed like an eternity ago he had had me up against this very counter. The memory of his lips on my throat sent a ghost of warmth through my battered body. I had been able to lose myself completely in the sensation of joining with him then, and right now, forgetting about everything for a couple of hours seemed like the perfect idea. Tomorrow was plenty early enough to start thinking again.

"Marcus," I called softly.

He looked back over his shoulder at me, one eyebrow raised ever so slightly in question.

"Come."

He obeyed, somewhat to my relief—I was way too sore everywhere to climb off the counter and walk over to him myself. Now that the last of my adrenaline had left my system I was all too keenly aware of the dull throbbing in every part of my body from Leo's abuse.

When Marcus was within reach, I put my hand on his chest and slid my palm up to his shoulder in a gentle caress before I curved it around his neck and pulled him down to me.

He let me guide him, though from the faint resistance in his body, I could tell he wasn't sure what I was doing. When our lips connected, however, it seemed to click.

His hands came up to rest around my back, and he brushed his lips gently against mine once, twice, three times until I arched my neck back to lead him to the sensitive spots there.

Marcus hesitated for just a moment, then obliged me.

His lips on my throat sent sharper tendrils of arousal down my spine and into my thighs, causing my muscles to contract and pain from my many bruises to bloom up through them. I winced, and Marcus paused, his lips hovering just above my skin.

"Where does it hurt?"

"Everywhere," I said, sliding my hand up to his jaw to try to pull him back. "It doesn't matter."

He made a rumbling sound deep in his throat and drew away from me. "It matters."

Irritation washed over me, dampening my growing arousal. "Why? You want a baby—this is how they're made. Let's just... get started."

Gently, he raised a hand to skim the tips of his fingers over my eye and cheekbone where Leo had hit me. "Take off your clothes."

Finally, we were getting somewhere. I shrugged out of my jacket, undid the buttons on my shirt, and pulled it off a little stiffly. The pants were harder, but I managed without aggravating any of my bruises too much, and after a few minutes I sat in just my bra and panties in front of him.

Marcus reached out for me again, and I thought he was going to slip my bra straps off my shoulders—until he gently pressed two fingers against a bruise on my clavicle.

"*Ow*," I whimpered, flinching from the unexpected touch. "What are you doing?"

"Seeing if you need a doctor," he said calmly, his eyes fixed on my body—but there was no fire in them, just clinical focus.

"I don't need a doctor!" I snapped, though I wasn't

sure how true that was. I hadn't taken much time to look over the damage Leo had done, but I figured that since I hadn't collapsed yet, I probably wasn't going to die.

Marcus ignored my anger and trailed his fingers down my body, testing every inch of it with light pressure.

I groaned in pain when he got to my stomach and hips where Leo had taken out most of his fury, but despite the discomfort, my frustration slowly began to wither. It had been a long time since anyone had taken the time to care for me like this, and there was something very soothing about letting Marcus tend to me so thoroughly. My mind wandered back to how he had painstakingly pulled every shard of glass from my raw feet when he saw the blood on my sock. Who would have thought the man capable of utter carnage, whose sheer presence spoke of danger and violence, would be so gentle with me?

"Do you do this to all the girls you get naked?" I asked when he was hunched down looking over my shins and calves. "Because someone should have told you you're playing doctor wrong. Just saying."

Unsurprisingly, he ignored me. Only when he had checked every inch of my body did he finally return his gaze to mine, straightening as he rose. "You're very tough."

"Thanks?" I arched an eyebrow at him. If there was one thing I didn't feel after today, it was tough.

"I'll make some food," he said, ignoring my questioning tone. I assumed that meant I didn't need a doctor.

"I just want to sleep," I said, frowning at his back as he

returned to the fridge. After his thorough, but kinda detached examination, I was no longer feeling particularly amorous, but his attentiveness had soothed me so much the exhaustion finally overwhelmed my mind, numbing out all the horrors almost as efficiently as a dose of endorphins could have. All I wanted was to pass out in a soft bed and sleep for as long as humanly possible.

"When did you eat last?" he asked without looking away from the fridge.

"This morning. But I'm really not hungry. Could you please just help me down? I don't want to land on my feet."

Without looking at me Marcus pulled an assortment of food from the fridge and then proceeded to retrieve crockery from the cabinets.

Apparently, I was eating whether I wanted to or not.

# ELEVEN

## MARCUS

*"Marcus."*

My cocoon of all-encompassing darkness rippled at the sound of the female voice, calling from somewhere beyond the monsters circling me.

I spun, searching frantically for the source of it, but all I saw were bloody entrails and brain matter. I looked down at my hands, already knowing what I'd find. They were soaked in blood, a knife clutched in one of them.

*I am the monster.*

Terror lanced through me and I roared in anguish, my voice no longer human. I was changing, becoming part of the monsters lurking in the shadows around me, and there was nothing I could do to stop it.

*"Marcus! Wake up. It's just a dream. Wake up!"* The darkness rippled again, more violently this time, and then

a pair of warm arms closed around me in a protective circle of light. *"Wake up."*

I came to with a gasp as the nightmare's death grip finally released me. Unexpected brightness made me squint, my eyes struggling to adjust even as I scrambled to sit up. Breathing deeply through my nose to try and calm my racing pulse, I buried my face in my hands and let the horrors of the dream slip away.

"Are you okay?" The unexpected sound of a female voice made me jolt and spin around, only to come face to face with a concerned-looking Evelyn.

I blinked, my heart rate slowly settling again as I took in her messy hair and green eyes lined with dark circles. She was the one who had called for me, had broken through my nightmare to wake me up, just as she had the night before. A rush of longing swept through me as I looked at her sitting in my bed, wearing one of my much too big t-shirts. Without pausing I reached out and pulled her against me, reveling in her feminine scent and softness.

She made a startled sound, but didn't struggle as I laid back down with her sprawled across my bare chest.

She felt just as perfect in my arms as she had the first time we'd shared a bed, and just like it had then, I felt all the tension in my body drain to the beating of her heart.

"What did you dream?" she asked, tilting her head to look up at me.

I never spoke about my nightmares. I never spoke

about any of the things that twisted in my broken mind. But...

"I was turning into a monster."

"Oh." Evelyn was silent for a little while, then added, "And it scared you?"

I grimaced at the ceiling. "Yes. I killed someone."

"Killing *scares* you?" she asked, the note of incredulity unmistakable. Not that I could blame her. She'd seen me after the monster had taken over.

"Someone innocent," I said, burying my nose in her hair to inhale her scent when the sick, ghostly vestiges of the dream threatened to wrap around me again. "It's always someone innocent."

"Oh." Her small hand came up to rest against my chest, and I closed my eyes and pretended like she was caressing me when her fingertips brushed over my skin in the process. Right now, I didn't care that I knew I couldn't trust her. All that mattered was that holding on to her made my broken mind stop its spiral.

"Do you have that dream often?"

"Every time," I said. The softness of her hair against my face felt so good. I rubbed my nose into it.

"Every time you kill?" The quaver of her voice betrayed her reluctance to bring up the subject of my nature. But I knew now that she was not as innocent as I'd thought. She knew about the world I lived my cursed existence in, had been part of London's underworld long enough to understand true darkness. She knew about violence and she knew about murder. She knew about me.

"Every time I lose control."

Evelyn didn't answer, but from her stiffness I knew she remembered what had happened in the basement I'd found her in, even if I barely remembered myself. There was only the black rage when I saw that filthy bastard try to force himself on her, the satisfaction of ripping his body apart and the absolute terror in Evelyn's eyes as she watched me do it. I had regained control sometime after that and found Liam and Louis waiting outside the door for me to calm down. The twins, like the rest of the Family, knew to keep their distance when the monster was in control.

"Sing to me," I said, finally lifting my nose from Evelyn's hair to let my head sink back into the pillow. Tonight was not the time to mull over the implications of Brigs' betrayal and Leo's death. Tomorrow would have to suffice.

Evelyn hesitated, and I could practically feel her urge to ask me why. To my relief, she didn't. "What do you want me to sing?"

"Don't care," I said, closing my eyes against the dim light. "I just want to hear your voice."

"Okay," she whispered, her breath ghosting across my chest.

I fell asleep to the sound of a lullaby I hadn't heard since my mother was still alive.

WHEN I WOKE up the next morning, Evelyn was gone.

Anger and betrayal welled up within me like a sour flood as I sat up and looked around for some trace of her. There was none, save the ruffled bedding next to me.

Had she played me again? What was it about that woman that made me such a fucking fool? She had already proven she would lie to get what she wanted from me, and still I'd expected her to keep to our deal. *Stupid!*

I tore out of the bed, intent on hunting her down and bringing her back. *Fine.* If she wanted to be locked up like a prisoner, that was exactly what she was going to get.

It took me less than ten seconds to throw on a t-shirt and pants, and I stalked out of the bedroom with dark anger bubbling in my chest. I was so intent on my purpose that the scene that met me in the living room didn't register until I was halfway to the door.

"Are you going somewhere?" Evelyn looked up from her perch on the sofa, a spoon of yogurt halfway to her mouth. She was still wearing the t-shirt I'd given her to sleep in, and my flat screen TV was turned on, though the volume was off. She was watching cartoons.

Something settled inside my chest, the anger evaporating and leaving an odd feeling of contentment in its place.

"I hope I didn't wake you? I kept the volume off because I didn't know if the sound would carry," she continued, putting down the bowl of yogurt as a small frown formed on her face. "Is something wrong?"

A small pang of longing curled in my gut. This was exactly the kind of scenario I wanted to wake up to more than I wanted anything else. My own little family enjoying breakfast, a woman who loved me and a child no one would ever take away from me either growing in her belly or sitting on the couch next to her. Seeing Evelyn still disheveled from sleep and wearing my shirt, on my couch and eating my food, was so close to what I yearned for with all my body and all my soul that I could nearly forget she was only here because of our agreement.

I took a step toward her, wanting more than anything to join her on the couch, but the look of alarm on her face stopped me cold.

"Marcus?"

I clenched my hands hard to stem the wave of bitter disappointment threatening to crash over me. I was being foolish. I knew what effect I had on people—I scared them just by being there. And Evelyn wasn't here because she could eventually come to love me. No one could. She was here because I could protect her.

"How are your injuries?" I asked, managing to force a neutral tone.

Evelyn shrugged, grimacing as she did. "I mean, I won't be doing any wild gymnastics anytime soon, but I'm still not dying, so... I'd class it as a win."

"Your feet?" I glanced down at the bandages.

"Pretty sore," she said, stretching her legs out a little and flexing her toes. She winced, that little experiment clearly having pushed her body too far.

"I'll look them over again," I said, turning around to fetch the First Aid kit from the bathroom.

She made noises behind me about it not being necessary, but gave up when I disappeared from view.

When I came back with fresh bandages and more ointment, she didn't bother to protest and obediently held out a foot as I shoved the coffee table out of the way to kneel in front of her.

The sole was still raw, but there was no sign of infection. I rubbed more salve on the multitude of cuts, being careful not to be too rough, and then put on a fresh bandage. With a little luck she should be back to normal soon.

"How do you know how to do this?" she asked as I began to unwrap her other foot. "I mean... I kind of assumed you were like Brigs. Mafia. Not someone who knows how to take care of injuries like this."

I breathed in deep to control the burst of anger at being compared to Brigs. I may be a monster, but I would never let a woman be tortured to death, nor would I ever hurt one. Even if she had betrayed both me and the Family, it would seem. I knew what my father would do, should he ever find out I had spared the life of a woman who would steal information from us. Which was why he could never know.

"My family is in the same business," I said as I rubbed ointment into a cut that was slightly deeper than the rest. Evelyn flinched, her foot spasming from the pain, but she didn't try to pull away. "We have to do a lot of patching up on the job."

Her nose scrunched up and her mouth pulling into a line from the pain of my care. "I suppose that makes sense."

Without answering, I grabbed the fresh bandage to re-wrap her foot. For someone who had been working as a honey trap, she seemed more disturbed by the realities of living in the underworld than she should have been.

When I was done I wiped my hands in my jeans and got up, intending to leave her to her breakfast and cartoons.

"Thank you," she said softly, offering me a tentative smile. "You're really good at that."

I grunted dismissively—I'd had plenty of practice. But her smile warmed something inside of me, and I felt the urge to sit by her side again, just so I could be near it.

"Marcus... do you think it would be possible to drive by my flat and pick up some things?" she asked, pulling my attention from her smile. "I need my clothes and shampoo and stuff."

"No. We can get you new things. Brigs will know what's happened to his nephew by now—he might keep tabs on your flat."

Her smile faltered. "But.. I don't want new things. I

want *my* things. Please, I don't want to lose everything I own to that creep on top of everything else he's done to me."

I frowned. Why was she fighting me on this? I was simply trying to hold up my end of the bargain—protecting her. "They're just things."

"Have you ever heard of sentimental value?" she huffed. "I want my things. I'm sure you can keep me safe for the ten minutes it'll take to get in and out."

I gritted my teeth, my own irritation rearing its head. It was a somewhat uncommon emotion for me—I was used to anger, but frustration? Less so. Probably because no one ever dared to argue with me about anything.

"I said no."

# TWELVE

## MARCUS

I was still irritated an hour and a half later after having driven Evelyn back from her flat and carried her bags of clothes and books and God-knew-what-else that she'd deemed *"absolutely vital"* up to mine.

I still had no idea how the fuck she had made me give in in the end, but I suspected it had something to do with how she had batted her eyelashes and gently touched my arm.

Yeah, she was a honey trap, all right. I'd seen countless men fall for women with an agenda before, but being part of the experience was entirely new to me. The women who wanted something from me bad enough to pretend like they weren't scared of me had never been able to lure me like Evelyn.

It had to be that underlying attraction between us I'd been unable to ignore since the first time I saw her. I'd wanted her like I'd never wanted another person before, and even now, when I knew what she was capable of, every part of my body longed for the sweet relief of her closeness.

I clutched the steering wheel of my Porsche as the agitation warred with longing somewhere deep in my chest. Right now was not the time to think about Evelyn. I had a meeting to prepare for, and if I wasn't in the right headspace, things were going to go south very quickly.

The twins had informed my father of what I'd done to Leo, but had been wise enough to leave out the few details I'd shared with them. I was going to have to explain that someone we'd thought was our ally had tried to steal from me, without letting him know what he had tried to take. If my father ever caught wind of the existence of what was on that pen drive, I knew I was dead—and no one would be left to protect my remaining brothers from him.

MY FATHER'S house was as gloomy as always, with its dark wooden panels and memories I'd rather be without lurking in every corner.

Wesley, my father's most trusted man, nodded at me as I walked into the drawing room where my family waited. If I hadn't seen Blaine's Jaguar and Liam's Land Rover in the driveway, I wouldn't have known my brothers had arrived yet. There was usually lively chatter whenever the twins were present, but today I was met by eerie silence.

They were all there, my remaining three brothers, along with my father, who was pacing like a beast who'd outgrown the confines of his cage. He stopped when he saw me.

"About fucking time, Marcus," he growled. "I'd expected Louis and Liam to waltz in late for a meeting this important, not you. Especially not when you're the goddamn reason we're here."

"I had to run an errand." I glanced at the twins, looking for any sign they'd mentioned the truth behind why I might be running late. They knew there was a girl involved—that I'd killed Leo because he was hurting a woman. They hadn't asked for details and I hadn't volunteered them, but they were both smart enough to know there was more to it than that. They were apparently also smart enough to have a tracker on my phone. I narrowed my eyes at their identical, ginger heads. I hadn't had the presence of mind to question how they'd managed to find me because I'd been too busy with Evelyn, but now it dawned on me that I'd never given them an address. *Crafty fuckers.*

"Well, since you've finally deigned it worth your time to show up, perhaps you would like to start out by explaining why you murdered the nephew of one of our only remaining allies?" My father's face was expressionless as always, but the clipped tone spoke volumes about the amount of self-restraint he was affecting to remain so.

"He tried to steal from me," I said, turning my focus on my father. "Information. They've turned on us."

For once, my father's carefully schooled mask fell, incredulity taking its place. "He did *what?* What information?"

"Sensitive information. The kind they could have used to take us down." I'd carefully crafted my answer to what I'd known was an unavoidable question. It had to have enough truth to it that it justified my actions, but there also needed to be no hint of the exact content—or the method they'd used. My gut twisted at the thought of what my father would do to Evelyn if he ever found out she'd been involved.

My father stared at me for a long moment. Then his lips thinned, his eyes turning dark and dangerous. Had I been younger, I would have expected his belt to follow. The muscle memory of the pain he could inflict with that strip of leather made my hands clench and the monster inside snarl.

"I don't believe you," he said flatly. "The Brigses have been loyal to our family for decades. Whatever your reason for lying to me—"

"He's not lying," Blaine interrupted, effectively silencing the room. "Gerald tried to pull a fast one on me during a deal last year. He wasn't pleased that I caught him in it. I thought he understood what would happen if he ever stepped a toe over the line again. Apparently, I was wrong."

My father snapped his head around to glare at Blaine, and I felt a stab of fear for my older brother. He looked as relaxed and confident as ever, but he had to know that what he'd just admitted to was not likely to go down well with our father. He took even the remotest hint of insubordination to the extremest consequences, and Blaine had a wife and baby at home.

"*Explain,*" my father hissed, clearly on the edge of losing his infamous temper.

Blaine shrugged. "The deal was forty million and a shipment of automatic weapons for a development site up in Manchester. Turned out to be a sham. He was expecting me to find out when it was much too late to do anything about it without losing face. So, I took the shipment of automatics to him and reminded him not to mess with the Steels. Perhaps I should have been more thorough with my reminder if he thought it a good idea to try and steal from Marcus."

"And why, pray tell, am I only hearing about this now?"

"I handled it. It wasn't necessary to bother you with it. Brigs promised to let the deal go back and to behave—I expected no more trouble from him."

Our father stared at him for a moment longer before he turned his focus back to me. Apparently, he'd accepted the explanation.

I had a hard time keeping the shock off my face. In my entire life, I'd never known him to let an issue of this size just drop. Just what was going on between the two of them? I looked back at Blaine for a clue and caught him exchanging a loaded glance with one of the twins. Had they known about this issue with Brigs? What else were my brothers hiding from our father? And from *me*?

"You do, of course, understand that we would have been in a much better position if you'd simply detained Leo rather than turning him into mincemeat?" my father asked as he folded his arms across his chest.

I nodded. Killing Leo hadn't been a conscious choice —it had been an instinctive reaction to seeing him abuse Evelyn, and I'd lost control. But if given the choice, I'd have done it again. He had hurt her, badly, and tried to rape her. I would have killed a man who subjected a girl I didn't know to such treatment, let alone the woman who sang to me to appease my nightmares.

"That temper of yours is going to be the death of you," Father said with a scowl. "But I won't let it be the end of our Family, you understand? From now on, you call one of your brothers before you act on something like this and let them deal with it. There are going to be no more slip-ups."

He didn't have to verbalize the threat—it was clear from his tone and his cold stare. One more incident that brought trouble to the Family, and I wouldn't like the consequences. I briefly wondered if it would be enough for him to order my murder like he had Jeremy's.

"What are we going to do about Brigs?" Louis said as he took a step forward, carefully putting himself in between me and our father as we stared each other down.

"We can't let attempted theft go unpunished, even if Gerald wasn't going to avenge Leo's death. Which he will," Liam continued.

Our father let out a deep sigh. "No. We'll have to take him down. The problem is that he was our last bastion of solid support, so we'll have to keep it within the Family. You will all need to gather your crews—I'll handle the intel. Make sure everyone stays quiet and is ready for action. We'll have to act quick before this gets out to the wider community. If the rest of the underworld think we might be losing a powerful ally before he's been taken down, they might think to rise against us. God knows there's been enough muttering in the shadows for the last year." He shot Blaine a pointed look.

I never did understand how my brother got away with the stunt he pulled. He broke the only law in the underworld when he informed the cops on the people who had kidnapped his wife. That our father hadn't disowned him for bringing the Family into bad standing was baffling, to say the least.

"Fine," Blaine said, ignoring our father's stare. "We'll get our crews together. We'll wait for you to get in touch, and then we strike."

"Yes," our father agreed. "Is everyone clear? Then get

out—and don't any of you get into any more fucking trouble, you got it? We're stretched thin as it is."

I left without another word, seething on the inside as was so often the case after having interacted with my father. I hated him, had hated him since I was a kid, but he was the iron fist that held the Family together.

"Marcus."

I looked up from my path toward my car, raising an eyebrow in question at Blaine as he cocked his head at me and walked over to his car, which was parked at the far end of the driveway.

When I made it over to him, he was silent for a bit as his eyes followed Liam and Louis's exodus from the driveway.

"What information did Brigs try to steal?" he asked me.

I frowned. I'd half anticipated news of my nephew—the only thing he and I really communicated about. Which was a big improvement over how things had been before Aidan's birth, where we had hardly talked at all. Not that I was close with any of my brothers, but the twins tended to check in on me once in awhile.

"Why do you ask?" I said, carefully taking measure of his face. Did he know something? I doubted it—if any of my brothers knew what our father had done, they would not have shown up here today pretending like everything was fine. Unlike me.

Blaine's face was as neutral as ever when he said, "I

noticed you didn't specify when dad asked. Figured there might have been a reason."

I grunted. "Not the sort of thing he needs to know about."

"Is it the sort of thing I need to know about? Or Liam and Louis?"

"No." If they ever knew, our family would be broken forever.

I might have hated my father, might have spent most of my time watching out that he didn't hurt my remaining brothers like he had Jeremy, but my family was all I had. If it fell apart, I would have nothing left to keep the darkness from swallowing me whole.

# THIRTEEN

## EVELYN

When Marcus returned home later that evening, he looked like he was in a foul mood.

I'd managed to produce a half-edible pasta dish from the ingredients in his surprisingly well-stocked fridge, so when he came in the door like a brewing thunderstorm, I was sprawled on his sofa with my still-wrapped feet on his fancy glass coffee table and a plate of food balancing against my boobs.

I pulled my feet off the table and straightened up a bit, attempting to look more like the kind of high-class girl I assumed he usually spent his time with. A task that was made somewhat harder by the wine I'd spilled on my t-shirt and the pair of my favorite sweatpants I'd climbed into the moment he left the flat. I grimaced when I realized what a mess I must appear, hoping he wasn't regretting the deal he'd made for my company in return for his protection.

"You can't have that," he said the moment his eyes landed on the glass.

"Oh. I'm sorry, I didn't know it was off-limits." I flushed despite having only opened the bottle because he'd told me to help myself to anything in the kitchen before he'd left. The wine both looked and tasted expensive, though, so he probably hadn't meant for me to have it.

"It's not good for the baby," he said, his lips flattening in disapproval.

I blinked. Even if he had no idea about the stash of birth control pills I'd sneakily stuffed into my bag when we went to my flat, it wasn't like we'd even had condomless sex yet.

"I'm not actually pregnant," I reminded him pointedly. "And this is good wine. Want a glass?"

"You will be soon," he said with a small growl, as if his plans to knock me up when he deemed me healed somehow meant I had to lay off the wine right this second.

"Yeah, sure." I rolled my eyes and put my plate down so I could get up from the sofa. My feet ached when they connected with the floor, but they were already much better than they had been earlier. "Why don't you sit down? I made enough dinner for you too. Do you like CSI?"

He shot me an indecipherable look as I hobbled over

to the kitchen counter where I'd left a plate with his food under some tin foil, but I heard him sink down on the couch a moment later.

Good. Perhaps he wouldn't be a broody pain in the arse all night, then. I poured another generous glass of the fancy wine before I returned to the couch, bottle in tow.

Marcus wasn't watching the TV, though, I noticed when I put the plate and glass down in front of him—he was watching me, with an intensity in his stormy gaze that made me feel self-conscious and awkward. I sat down next to him and released my hair from the messy bun so it could cover the splotch of wine on my top.

"So... how was your day?" I asked, partly to make him stop staring at me and partly because I wanted to make up for the less-than-stellar start to the evening. While he'd been gone, I'd had plenty of time to think about what would happen to me if he grew tired of our arrangement and left me to fend for myself. It had left me with a stern resolve to be the best companion he could ever want, because I much preferred spending my days taking care of Marcus like some parody of a housewife than running into my former employer again.

Unfortunately for me, Marcus wasn't much of a small talker. He simply grunted at my question and then turned his focus to the pasta, grabbing his fork to dig in.

"Any news about Brigs?" I pressed, opting instead to try and pump him for news about the man who would undoubtedly be gunning for us both now.

Marcus, who had been mid-way through chewing his first bite of pasta, coughed violently and I saw him try to mask a grimace as he forced himself to swallow. He reached for the glass of wine and downed half of it in one go.

I felt my cheeks heat from his obvious distaste of my food. "I'm sorry. I suck so bad at cooking, I know. I'll do better."

"No, it's fine," he said a little too quickly, turning his gaze back to me. "Thank you. For leaving me some."

I narrowed my eyes at him, pretty sure he was lying. But why? If Marcus was anything, it was big and gruff and not at all the kind of guy who would lie about my horrible cooking to try and save my feelings. Right?

But as I saw him take another careful bite and almost succeed in masking his distaste as he chewed it, it was obvious that that's what he was doing. A small measure of warmth spread in my chest and I offered him a genuine smile. "Of course. It's part of the deal, isn't it? You protect me and I take care of you."

"Hmm," he hummed, taking another swig of the wine.

"So, Brigs?" I pressed, filling up his glass once he'd put it down.

"You don't need to worry about it," he said. "We'll take care of him."

" 'We' being your family?" I asked.

"Mmhm."

I frowned. "And you're okay just trusting your dad

with this? I mean, it was your dad on that video, wasn't it?"

Marcus' face darkened, and for a moment I thought he wasn't going to answer. But then he nodded, not taking his eyes off the terrible pasta. "It was."

"And... he had one of your brothers killed?" I said, trying to somehow make sense of what he was telling me. "And you and your other brothers don't even bat an eyelid?"

"They don't know," he said, his voice softer than before.

It took me a little while to fully process that little tidbit. "I'm sorry... you had a video of your father ordering a hit on one of your brothers, and you haven't told any of them? Why?"

Marcus' full lips pinched and I saw regret cross his features. And fear. It was an odd emotion to see on the otherwise tough man.

"I might not know a lot about what it's like to be a part of a big crime family, but that seems really wrong. Do you not get along with your brothers? What's to stop your dad from trying to kill one of them, if they cross him somehow?" Perhaps it was the glass of wine I had before Marcus came home that made me loose-lipped enough to air my shock, but the thought of hiding something this big from your family... I just couldn't comprehend how he could keep a secret like that.

"I won't let him hurt them," Marcus said, the gruffness

returning to his voice before he emptied the wine from his glass and put it down again. "That's why I kept that video. To blackmail him if he made a move against any of us."

The video I had destroyed. I swallowed thickly, suddenly not feeling too great about the direction of the conversation. "Marcus, I…"

"If you had refused Brigs, he would have hurt you." He sighed, putting the plate of nearly untouched pasta down on the table. "We made a deal—your debt to me will be paid in kind. I'll find another way to keep them safe."

I bit my lip, not entirely sure if I should be relieved he wasn't harboring a grudge, or deeply disturbed that he truly believed he was going to impregnate me. I settled on somewhere in between.

"You should tell them," I said, touching his shoulder lightly to draw his attention to me. "It's the best way you can protect them. Let them know they could be in danger. Your brother who has the baby—Blaine, was it? Shouldn't he be allowed to protect his own family?"

Marcus' jaw worked once, twice, before he looked at me. The agony in his stormy eyes took my breath away.

"It will splinter the Family," he said, his voice not much louder than a whisper. "What's left of it."

My heart clenched as I stared into his pained gaze. How often did Marcus Steel ever show any vulnerability? Never, was my bet. It was probably the wine that made him lower his barriers now, but it didn't lessen the impact. Without thinking I reached out and cupped my hand around his cheek, desperate to soothe the pain I saw.

"He *killed* your brother, Marcus. You telling the others won't splinter your family—he already did that. But it might make you able to glue some of the pieces back together. Think of that little kid," I nodded at Aidan's picture next to the TV. "You can't let someone that innocent grow up in a family where his own grandfather might hurt his dad."

In truth, I don't know why I was so adamant that he tell his brothers of their father's betrayal. It shouldn't have concerned me—I was only here for his protection. But as I stared into Marcus' eyes I felt the same draw as I had the first night we met. And I knew, despite everything, that I wanted this man to find peace.

Marcus looked at the silver-framed photo of his nephew for a moment. When he returned his focus to me, his eyes were dark with something else—something that made my heart skip a beat and my abdomen clench.

"You're right," he whispered, a hoarse note to his voice. "A child can't grow up like this. *Our* child can't grow up like this."

I blinked, not expecting that particular turn, but before I could voice an answer, Marcus' soft lips pressed against mine.

I groaned into his mouth when he separated his lips and teased at the seam of mine with his tongue for access, my body already giving in to the delicious warmth of him.

Perhaps it was the wine that made it so easy to wrap my arms around his neck and let him lay me down on the couch without a second thought to how swiftly the mood between us had changed. Where seconds ago my chest was tight with empathy for the big man currently pinning me to the sofa, it now flowed with warmth and just a trickle of excitement as his skilled lips danced over mine.

When he pushed my t-shirt up and bared my breasts, he finally broke our kiss to dip his head lower. I gasped and arched when Marcus closed his mouth around my right nipple, enveloping it in his heat. He swiped his tongue over the little bud until it pebbled under his ministrations and then sucked it deeply.

I whimpered, my fingers finding their way to his silky black hair of their own accord. I clenched my hands in his soft strands for every deep pull of his lips against my nipple until the stimulation became too much. But just as I was about to voice a complaint, Marcus popped his mouth off my now achingly erect nipple and gave me a deep kiss before he switched to the other.

I writhed underneath him, excitement mixing with rapidly mounting desire—a desire that crescendoed when he pushed a hand down my sweatpants and my panties, his fingers finding my clit without pausing to search.

"*Oh,*" I gasped, jerking hard underneath him at first contact, and again when he rubbed it none too gently. But it felt good, right—he wasn't terrified of breaking me like he had been the first night we'd spent together, but he was obviously still in control. My body melted, swept away by the maddening bursts of pleasure he elicited from my heated flesh. I grasped at his shirt, desperate to feel more of his skin, and he pulled off my breast so I could get at his buttons, though he never paused his ministrations between my thighs.

The fire in his eyes as he looked down at me made my pussy clench and wet heat flood from my aching core. I wanted him—I wanted all that barely leashed ferocity, all the burning lust and every inch of his powerful body. *God*, I wanted his body! I'd succeeded in getting his shirt open and was greeted by the sight of stack after stack of strong, lean muscle in his abdomen and a chest and arms so strong I wanted to lose myself in his embrace forever.

"You're beautiful," I whispered—and then gasped hoarsely when he, without warning, pulled my pants off my legs before he returned to my sex, this time pushing two fingers into me, his thumb taking over on my aching bundle of nerves. My pussy opened greedily for him, craving him ever deeper, and I arched my hips, lost to the feel of penetration. I wouldn't have been ready for it so swiftly with any other man, but Marcus made my body sing.

"No," he said, his voice so rough with lust it was like gravel. The sound of it went straight to my core and I felt myself pulse around his invading fingers. "*You* are beautiful, Evelyn. Every inch of you. I want our baby to look just like you."

I blinked at the distinctly unexpected strand of dirty talk, but was quickly distracted when he forced a third finger into me, making my walls spasm from the hard stretch. I moaned, half in protest, but just then he curved his fingertips into the spongy place on my frontal wall and everything went white with pleasure.

"I want to take you until your body gives in, until your womb is bathed in my seed. And then I want to see you grow round with my child. See your pregnant body writhe with pleasure when I make love to you over and over," he growled, never letting up on the firm pressure against my pulsing G-spot.

I cried out, too wrapped up in the intensity of his touch to object to what he was saying. And, as he fucked me with his fingers and told me how he couldn't wait to push into me and give me the baby he wanted so bad, I lost the will to protest. I came on his hand to the image of being round with child, *his* child, the ecstasy it brought sweeping me away like a torrent.

Marcus was on me before I could catch my breath, his fingers replaced by something bigger. Hotter. I wrapped my legs around his hips when he pushed in, hilting his cock in my still-fluttering pussy in one, smooth push.

"*Fuck!*" I whimpered as my channel struggled to adjust. He was so big even three of his fingers hadn't fully prepared me for the deep penetration nor the sensation of feeling his hot, bare skin skin inside of me for the first time, and I clutched at his shoulders to make him stop for just a moment.

Marcus obeyed my unspoken plea, holding still deep within me while my shuddering core grew accustomed to his presence. He peppered my jawline and throat with heated kisses, fanning the flames in my already smoldering body.

We both felt it the moment I was ready for more.

Marcus lifted up on his hands above me, holding most of his weight in his arms—and then he moved.

I mewled at the sensation of his hard cock sliding halfway out of my pussy, only to drive back in the next second. He took me in long, hard thrusts, grunting every time he bottomed out inside of me, driving moans and cries from my lips.

It wasn't like the first time we'd had sex. He wasn't overly gently, wasn't scared of hurting me anymore, but even though the savage fire in his eyes flamed with every stroke, he never lost his full grip on self-control.

Being underneath him, feeling him take me, was much like riding a barely tamed beast. I felt both supremely powerful and completely at his mercy. It was the most addictive experience in the entire universe.

When I began the climb for my second orgasm of the evening, Marcus was there with me. His hips, which had been pumping against me in strong, fluid motions, snapped down hard when I dug my fingernails into his shoulders and cried out in a wordless plea for more.

If I'd had any grip left on my conscience, I might have feared the minor pain would have snapped his self control once more, but I was mindless in my pursuit of the rush I knew lay just beyond my reach. I ground myself up against his body and cried out when he responded to my fervent demands by shoving his thick cock deep into me, pounding me over and over. I wailed in ecstasy and clung to him as I finally found my release. My mind flooded with endorphins and my body was alight with sensation as I gasped and cried out beneath the man who'd fucked me to completion like no one before him. I was only half-aware of his strangled groan of pleasure when he stilled inside of me, his fingers digging into my hips with bruising strength as the warm rush of his essence flooded into me.

Marcus collapsed on top of me, halfway squishing me into the softness of the couch, but I didn't mind. I felt warm and safe and so completely, perfectly at peace.

Even when Marcus nuzzled his face against the side of my head and murmured, "You'll make such a good mother," I felt nothing but blissful pleasure as I closed my eyes and let the afterglow whisk me away to a dreamless sleep.

# FOURTEEN

### EVELYN

The first thing I noticed when I woke up the next morning was that someone—I suspected Marcus—had carried me from the couch to the bed, and also gotten rid of the rest of my clothes before tucking me in.

The second thing I noticed was the sticky downside of having sex without a condom.

I groaned with equal measures of distaste and misery as I sat up in Marcus' wide king-sized bed, not entirely sure if the worst part of today was my wine headache or the residue of Marcus' attempt at impregnating me.

Grunting, I scrambled out of bed, noticing first that Marcus was missing and then the glass of water and two aspirins on the nightstand by my side.

I swallowed both in three large gulps, sending the big brute a thankful thought as the painkillers slipped down my throat. Feeling mildly better already, I grabbed a fresh change of clothes from the weekend bag I'd packed when he took me to my flat and then shuffled toward the bathroom, intent on not looking like something a fraternity spat out after a long weekend.

Marcus' bathroom was as luxurious and sparse as the rest of his flat, with black marble, glass and chrome dominating all surfaces, and I spent a good twenty minutes in the shower just letting the water wash away my headache and Marcus' semen. When I wrapped myself in one of his fluffy towels after, I felt like a new person.

Unfortunately, when I lifted off the top of the toilet to reach for the plastic baggy stuffed full of birth control pills I'd hidden there the second Marcus left yesterday, my good mood vanished pretty instantaneously. The cistern was empty. Or, it had water and all the thingamajigs a water cistern should have, but there was no trace of my plastic bag, nor my pills.

I stared at the place the bag should have been safely tugged away as my brain went over every possible scenario that could have led to my birth control pills just up and walking out of there on their own. Unfortunately, it wasn't having much luck, and I pressed both hands to my face with a groan when I finally accepted the truth.

Somehow, Marcus had been one step ahead of me.

*"You'll make such a good mother,"* he'd said last night. I'd assumed it was just a wrap-up of the weird pregnancy fetish thing he'd had going while we were making love, but no. The bastard had probably seen me sneak it into

my bag when we were at my flat and planned to pilfer it when I was zonked out on my orgasm high. *Fuck!*

I stared down at my abdomen, suddenly having the oddest sensation of carrying around a ticking time bomb in my ovaries. This whole deal had been easy enough to agree to when I'd thought there was no way he was going to get me pregnant anyway, but now...? How the hell was I going to avoid ending up carrying his baby now?

A vague memory from last night brushed through my mind—the faintest whisper of the things Marcus had said about seeing me pregnant, and for a second I imagined myself swollen with his child. What it would feel like to have a little one to care for—and a man like Marcus to share it with.

*Yeah, because getting pregnant with a mafia son's child —a mafia son you've known for a grand total of two days, no less—would be the best idea ever.* I mentally slapped myself, hard, until whatever idiotic seed all Marcus' baby talk had planted in my brain withered and died. Two days ago I'd thought of the man as a monster, and while I was beginning to understand that that was far from the truth, I also wasn't some harebrained girl looking to settle down with the first man with enough cash to want a dedicated housewife.

I pressed a hand to my abdomen and refocused on my more immediate problem. I'd managed to take a pill yesterday, so as far as I understood basic biology, last night's sexcapades wouldn't end up with a surprise pregnancy. Which meant my problem was just moving forward—and ensuring I didn't fall for Marcus' devious lips and that innate fire that went straight to my ovaries whenever he looked like he wanted to devour me.

All right. With some planning, a lot of self-control, and a good heap of luck, I might be able to get through this without giving in to Marcus' demands for a baby.

*Damn that man.*

I got dressed, wrapped my feet as best I could on my own, and left the bathroom, and when I heard noises of pots and pans and detected the delicious scent of bacon spreading through the penthouse, I steered myself in the direction of the kitchen. I found Marcus in front of the stove, wearing a t-shirt and jeans. His feet were bare, and when he spotted me, he offered a relaxed smile. "Morning."

I narrowed my eyes at him, forcing the softness in my heart back when I realized it was the first time I'd seen him look so... content. The cloud of darkness that usually loomed behind his gray gaze was nowhere in sight.

"Yeah, morning to you too. Quick question—when we made that deal about me being your companion in return for your protection... you really only cared about the baby part, didn't you?"

He shrugged as he stirred what looked like a pan-full of scrambled eggs.

"You're a real arse," I growled. "You can't just force me to have your kid—it's not the fucking forties."

"I'm not forcing you. You agreed to the deal." Despite my crass language, he remained infuriatingly calm.

I balled my hands into fists by my sides, hating that he was right. He hadn't forced me... I just hadn't had much of a choice if I wanted to not get horrifically murdered by Brigs. Part of me wanted to push him, to demand what he'd do if I refused to have sex with him again, but the smarter part thankfully shut that down before I opened my mouth. I didn't much relish the thought of spending my foreseeable future locked up in a basement somewhere.

I sat down on the bar stool by the kitchen island and glared at his perfect, broad back while he continued cooking what looked like would end up as a full English breakfast. Mid-glare, my gaze snagged on the black phone that lay on the island just within my reach. *His* phone.

A stab of vengeance made me reach for it as inconspicuously as I could, and to my surprise I managed to snatch it without him noticing. I swiped the screen and was greeted by a picture of a tall, dark-haired man who looked a lot like Marcus with his arm around a small woman with chestnut hair, a happy smile, and a baby in her arms that looked a lot like the one in the frame by the TV. It had to be his brother, Blaine, and his family.

*Hmm.* I hadn't had much of a plan when I grabbed his phone apart from just violating his privacy a bit as petty revenge for him getting rid of my birth control, but the image of his brother made me remember our talk last night, before things got... carnal.

I wondered if he'd been in touch with Blaine, or any of his other brothers while I was sleeping, and flicked my way into his call logs. Nothing since yesterday. I found my way to his texts and scrolled through them. Nothing there, either. In fact, when I snooped a bit further, all his texts were one-word answers to someone else texting him a time or a place, either confirming or denying.

I recalled the fear and pain in his eyes when he'd talked about his family being splintered if they found out, and my heart broke for him all over again. But if he didn't do this... I'd only known him for a few days and he might be trying to get me pregnant despite my obvious reluctance, but one thing I was sure of was that I didn't want him to be hurt by the gruesome man I'd seen in that video.

I scrolled through his contacts and found the one marked *"Blaine"*. With skilled swiftness I typed, *"Can you come by today? We need to talk about dad."* and hit *"send"* before I quickly slid the phone back to its original position.

The small sound it made against the marble made Marcus turn around, his questioning expression turning into mistrust as he looked from me to his phone. "Did you touch my phone?"

I shrugged, pretending like the sudden darkening of his handsome features wasn't scary in the least. "Maybe."

*"Evelyn."* There was an unmistakable warning in his

deep voice, and my attempt at bravado cracked like an egg.

"I texted your brother and asked him to come by."

Marcus stared at me as if he wasn't sure I'd lost my mind.

"You said you'd tell them about your dad, but when I looked, you hadn't been in contact with anyone. I'm just making sure you don't make a mistake you can't take back because you're afraid," I explained, and then paled when I realized what I'd said. I'd commented on the moment of weakness he'd shown me last night, and judging from the way Marcus' nostrils pulled up, it wasn't appreciated.

"That was not for you to do," he growled, and I could see the anger flickering behind his gray eyes. He no longer looked content, and I felt a stab of guilt. I pushed it aside and returned his dark look, pushing out my jaw to steel myself.

"Were you going to do it? Honestly? And if you were, when? I know it's a big deal, and I know it's none of my business. But I saw what was on that video, Marcus. I may not know your family, but I know a man capable of truly despicable things when I see one. Your dad... he could choose to hurt any of your brothers and you might be too late to stop it. He could choose to hurt *you*. You know this needs to happen, I know you do." I slid off the bar stool and walked the few steps around the kitchen island so I could reach out for him, placing my hand against his warm arm.

He stared down at me, at where my hand was touching his skin. "Why do you care?" he asked, lifting his burning gaze to mine. "Why do you care what happens to me, or to my family?"

I swallowed thickly, unable to look away from his eyes. Why *did* I care? It wasn't just the guilt of how I'd deceived him to steal that video from him, that much I was pretty sure of. I'd done much worse to other men while working for Brigs, even if he was the first I'd gone all the way with. But then what was it? The weird pull I'd felt toward him from the first time we'd met?

Was it the fact that, behind the darkness and danger that radiated off him and kept everyone else at bay, I'd seen the gentleness and longing he kept so closely guarded? That he was the only one who had gone out of his way to care for me and protect me since my mother got sick?

"You're a good person," I said softly. "You don't deserve to carry all that pain on your own."

Marcus stared down at me for the longest time before he finally said, "I'm not a good person, Evelyn. I'm a monster."

The way he said it, so calmly, it almost masked the flicker of pain in his eyes, made my heart break for him. Hadn't I thought the same thing, when I saw him tear Leo apart? He'd been an animal, slave to his rage, and he'd scared me so much I'd run as fast as I could to get away. But what he'd done, he'd done to the man who'd hurt me.

Despite my initial fear of him, I'd felt safe in his hands since the first night we spent together. I'd felt safe enough to offer him my companionship, and I'd gratefully taken the protection of his presence in return. As I looked up at him, I realized I felt safe with him because that's exactly what I was.

"You're not a monster. Whatever else you are, you're not that. Even after what I did to you, you're still making sure Brigs won't hurt me again. No monster would do that." I gave his arm a squeeze and offered him a faint smile. "And no monster would have his brother's family as his phone's background."

Marcus looked at me in silence for a long moment before he gently grabbed my chin and tipped my head up. For a second I thought he was going to kiss me, and my heart sped up until I could feel it beating hard against my ribs. But he just searched my eyes, an expression of curiosity and something I couldn't decipher playing across his handsome face.

A sharp beep from his phone shattered the moment. Marcus let go of my face and grabbed the phone, and I drew in a shuddering mouthful of air, realizing I'd been holding my breath.

"What is it?" I asked when a small frown formed between Marcus' eyebrows.

"Blaine's coming over in an hour," he said, not taking his eyes off the phone. "To talk about our father."

# FIFTEEN

## EVELYN

I don't know why, but the knowledge that I was about to meet one of Marcus' family members made butterflies the size of albatrosses take up residence in my stomach.

I spent the first half hour dashing around the flat trying to figure out how to make myself useful, and finally settled on filling the dishwasher and putting on a load of laundry. Perhaps it was Marcus' brooding energy that set my nerves on edge, or maybe it was the knowledge that I didn't quite know how he was going to introduce me to his brother—and if he went with *"This is the girl Brigs hired to steal from me,"* I wasn't entirely sure his protection would extend to shield me from his family's wrath.

"What are you doing?"

I stopped wiping down of the sink and looked over my shoulder at Marcus, who had lifted his head for the first time since he got Blaine's text.

"Cleaning?" I gave the cloth in my hand a shake for emphasis. "We're getting company in a second." And also, it was what I did when I was nervous.

He arched an eyebrow at me. "You don't need to do that."

"I'm pretty sure that's what my part of the deal is," I countered. "I'm your companion, if you recall. Isn't cleaning and cooking part of the job?"

"It's not. Come here."

Hesitantly, I obeyed, putting the cloth down by the sink. When he motioned for me to take a seat on the bar stool next to him, I did. "Then what am I here for?"

"Company," he said as he bent to snatch up one of my feet. He lifted it up in his lap and gave the bandages a careful inspection. "You shouldn't be on your feet so much."

"They're much better already," I said, and then sighed when he undid the strip of gauze to adjust it. "You're fussing."

Marcus only grunted in reply, and then grabbed my other foot so he could fix that bandage too.

I watched him work, his large hands surprisingly nimble and gentle as he wrapped my damaged feet, and I wondered if he meant that I was here for company, or if it was just a nice way of saying that all he really wanted from me was to breed me like livestock.

A knock on the door startled me. Instinctively, I pulled on the foot still locked in Marcus' grasp.

He gave me an admonishing look before he finished wrapping the bandage, ensuring it was exactly how he wanted it. Only then did he get up from the stool and walk over to open the door.

The man on the other side was nearly as tall as Marcus, with the same shade of black hair and approximately the same wide build. He was also flanked by a short woman with a fussy toddler in her arms. I recognized them all from the picture on Marcus phone and frowned. Seemed Blaine had brought his family.

"Mira," Marcus said. He sounded surprised too, but nevertheless bent to brush a kiss against her cheek and press one to the head of the toddler.

"Hi, Marcus," she chirped happily, and then shoved the kid into his arms without preamble. "He's been a right pain this week. I think he's teething again."

The baby gurgled and twisted in Marcus' arms, dropping the rattle he'd been happily chewing on to grasp at his uncle with both hands.

"Who's this?" the man in the door asked, his eerily familiar gray eyes zeroing in on me. They looked so much like Marcus', only without the looming darkness. It wasn't that Blaine didn't look like he could be pretty damn dangerous if you crossed him, but there wasn't the same viciousness just behind the surface.

"Oh, hello!" the woman—Mira—said, her head popping up as she finally spotted me. She'd been focused on her kid and Marcus up until then.

Marcus looked at me across his shoulder for a moment before turning back to his brother and sister-in-law. "Evelyn. My fiancée," he said, as if he'd just announced the weather. Still with the baby in his arms he stepped back so the two in the doorway could come in.

It took both of them a moment to move. They stared at Marcus in silence for a moment, both looking suitably stunned, before Mira managed to pull herself together and give her husband a nudge with an elbow as she stepped all the way into the flat.

"I didn't even know you were seeing anyone. Congratulations!" A wide smile took over her dumbfounded expression, and she raised up on her tiptoes to press a kiss to Marcus' cheek before she turned her attention to me. "It's very nice to meet you, Evelyn. I'm Mira—Blaine's wife."

I managed to come out of my own stupor in time to slide off the bar stool and accept the hug she pulled me into. "I guess I'm the first to tell you welcome to the family? The twins would have definitely told us if they'd met you."

"Thank you," I croaked, shooting a bewildered look at Marcus—who was too busy making sure the baby didn't escape to pay me any mind. Apparently, letting me know beforehand that he wanted me to play his fiancée in front of his family hadn't been worth mentioning.

"Yes. Welcome to the family."

I looked up just in time to see Blaine approach,

pulling me in against his leather coat with one arm for a brief moment. He looked at me with slightly narrowed eyes, as if he was trying to work out if I was a threat of some sort.

"Marcus, you asked me to come so we could talk," he said, and from his tone I guessed he wasn't too pleased with having a stranger present.

"I did." Marcus shot me a sideways glance I pretended I didn't notice. With a small sigh he handed the kid back to its mother and gestured toward the kitchen island. "We should sit."

Blaine shot me another look. "Perhaps this is something we should discuss in private."

Marcus arched an eyebrow at him, and something close to defensiveness crossed his features. "Then why did you bring your wife?"

"Because she knows about him," Blaine countered, crossing his arms over his chest. "And you trust her as much as you trust me."

Mira grimaced. "This is not a way to treat your brother's wife-to-be." She sent Blaine a stern look and then turned to me. "Why don't we go into the bedroom for some, ah, girl talk while they chat?"

I was more than okay with missing a conversation between the two brothers about their father murdering a third son and gave Mira a grateful smile, but before I could accept, Marcus' voice cut through.

"Evelyn stays here. And I would prefer if you do, too,

Mira. This concerns you and Aidan as much as it does me and Blaine."

Mira's expression fell and she exchanged a look with her husband as she shifted the toddler to one hip. "All right, then. I guess we better stay."

Blaine shot me another glance, clearly not thrilled by my presence, but relented with a sigh. "Fine. If you trust her, so will I."

Marcus nodded, his lips pinching as he leaned against the kitchen island. Mira sat down next to me, but Blaine remained standing by her side, resting a hip against the counter with his arms folded across his chest.

"Am I correct in assuming this has got something to do with the information Brigs tried to steal?" Blaine said after a moment's loaded silence, save Aidan's small noises.

"Yes," Marcus said, his voice softer than usual. "I had a video of dad ordering Wesley to kill Jeremy. Brigs wanted it, probably to blackmail us."

Shocked silence followed his words. I glanced from Mira to Blaine. Her face flashed with bitter anger before she put her toddler-free hand on her husband's back in silent support. Blaine looked stunned for a moment. Then grief, and finally anger, passed over his handsome features.

"He killed Jeremy? When?"

"Two years ago."

"Just before he supposedly traveled to the States,"

Blaine said, his voice hard. "I take it he never actually left London?"

"I don't know. I didn't see the tape before dad told us Jeremy had left. I tried to get in touch with him, but..."

"But he never responded to any communication," Blaine finished, rubbing his hand over his face. "*Fuck.*"

"You need to tell him about Isaac, my love," Mira said quietly as she stroked her husband's back a few times.

Marcus stiffened, and I saw the briefest flicker of anguish pass over his face before he schooled it into its usual calm mask. "Is he dead, too?"

"No," Blaine said gruffly. "He's still in jail—exactly where Dad put him. He set him up to take the fall for that drug bust—Isaac refused to kill someone, and Dad punished him for it by getting him locked up."

"Dad was worried Jeremy would usurp him," Marcus said. "That's why he had him killed. If he put Isaac in jail for disobeying him, I take it you have some sort of hold over him since he hasn't punished you for saving Mira last year?"

*Saving Mira?* My eyes flickered to the auburn-haired woman, a brief moment of curiosity making me wonder what had happened last year that required saving her, but now wasn't the time to ask. There were far more pressing problems to address.

"He knows I know about Isaac," Blaine said. "I told him I would tell you and the twins—and Jeremy—if he crossed me. I didn't know he was capable of... murdering one of us."

"Do you have the video, Marcus?" Mira asked. "I'd like to see it."

I cringed and sent Marcus a pleading look, but he didn't even glance in my direction.

"It got destroyed when Brigs tried to steal it," he said, thankfully choosing not elaborating on how.

"That's why you decided to tell me?" Blaine guessed. "Because you can't use it as blackmail if he decides to go after one of us."

Marcus nodded shortly, his face as dark as ever. "We have to stop him."

Blaine rubbed his hands across his face again with a grunt. "Yeah. We do. But the timing is terrible. With Brigs sniffing at our heels, we won't survive it if we turn on each other now." He paused, clearly mulling something over. "We need to wait until Brigs has been taken care of, but we have to warn the twins. Let them know to watch their backs. When Brigs has been dealt with, we will find a solution. Together."

"And Isaac?" Marcus asked.

Blaine sighed. "If we can. He's refused visitors the entire time he's been in there, and this is not the sort of thing I want to write a letter about. Plus, I doubt Dad's going to see him as a threat as long as he's locked up. Let's tell the twins and then bide our time."

Marcus nodded again as he drew in a deep breath.

"All right." His gaze slid to Aidan on Mira's hip. "If there's any sign of trouble, you got an exit strategy for them?"

Blaine snorted and pushed off the kitchen counter. "Since the day she got back to me." The look he shared with his wife was so soft and filled with love I felt like I was suddenly intruding on an intimate moment. He reached out and wrapped his arm around her shoulder, pulling her up from the bar stool and close against his body.

"We should get back. I'm prepping my crew for the Brigs thing and need to get in touch with a few people. And you," he nodded at me. I'd more or less assumed I'd been forgotten about in the middle of the sombre family moment. "If you love my brother enough to marry into this shit show, then you make him give you my number. If there's any trouble and he isn't around, don't hesitate to call. Got it?"

I nodded, not trusting my voice, but he didn't seem to notice or care. Instead he turned to Marcus and clasped his free hand on his shoulder. "Get in touch with the twins. I think they'll take it better coming from you."

Mira offered me a brief smile as they left, but her face was drawn with tension. Not that I could blame her—being involved in a double mafia Family showdown was terrifying enough for me—I couldn't imagine what it would be like to have a baby to protect in the middle of it all.

I turned to Marcus once the door had been closed.

"Thank you for not telling them I was the one who tried to steal the video for Brigs."

He shrugged. "It wasn't important."

"I guess they wouldn't have trusted me as easily if they knew," I said, feeling a stab of guilt. Even from our brief interaction I sensed that they were both good people —as good as members of a crime family can be, anyway.

Marcus grunted. I took that as confirmation.

"Might also have been harder to sell the whole 'fiancée' thing, I suppose." I frowned at him. "Why did you lie about that, anyway?"

"I didn't lie," he said, not even bothering to look in my direction. "I'm marrying you."

## SIXTEEN

MARCUS

"Excuse me, you're *what?*"

Evelyn's sharp tone drew my thoughts from the conversation I'd just had with Blaine—and that I'd need to have with the twins. Her pretty face was screwed up in shock and her skin was looking pinker than usual.

"Hmm?"

"You're *marrying* me?" she said, her voice hiking up at the end.

"Yes."

The light pink in her cheeks turned dark and splotchy. "I don't recall that being part of the deal we made."

"No."

Her green eyes narrowed. "You can't change the rules like that."

I frowned at her irate expression. "It's got nothing to do with our deal. I'm not changing the terms."

"I'm not marrying you!" she hissed.

"Yes, you are."

"You can't fucking force me to marry you. What's wrong with you?" she screeched, opting for the higher part of her voice's register this time. "Stupid deal or not, I'm not something you own!"

I cocked my head as I took in her ire, trying to work out what had angered her. Even carrying the weight of my father's deceit, seeing Evelyn this upset pushed other concerns aside as the monster in my chest raised its head as if to sniff out the cause so it could annihilate it. I pushed it down and focused on the small woman in front of me. Every part of me longed to reach out and hold her tight, but I knew we weren't familiar enough for her to accept my comfort. She accepted more carnal kinds of intimacy readily enough, but I knew there was a difference. I'd had sex with women before and never experienced the urge to wrap my arms around them and never let go. Not the way I did with Evelyn.

"I won't force you," I said, hoping that misunderstanding was the cause for her anger.

Both her eyebrows shot up high on her forehead. "Oh? Perhaps you would like explain why I'd marry you, then?"

"You'll marry me because we belong together," I said, the magnitude of saying out loud what I'd known since the first time I saw her sending a rush of pleasure through my body. I had tried to deny it, tried to rein in my overwhelming need for her with the knowledge that the darkness in me would destroy her like it had me. But when I'd seen her helpless in Leo's hands and the anger welled up to consume me, I'd known—even when I lost my mind to the monster, I could never hurt her. Everyone else, but not her. Even the monster wanted to protect her. Be with her.

And so when she'd offered her companionship for my protection I'd accepted, because I knew she was strong enough to not let my darkness taint her. I had asked for a child because even when she left me again, I would still have part of her with me. Part of what could have been. Someone I could love until the end of time. Someone who might love me, too.

It wasn't until she looked into my eyes and called me a good person that I knew I would never survive if she walked away. She was the only one in the world who saw more than the monster when she looked at me, and I couldn't lose her. Not when I'd finally found her—when I'd finally felt a shimmer of what it was like to be whole again.

Evelyn blinked, her mouth dropping to a pouty little "O" as some of the anger on her face was replaced with shock.

"W-what do you mean?" Even her voice was lower, hoarser, than before.

I couldn't resist reaching for her—touching her. I cupped her cheek and felt the usual buzz of elation when my skin touched hers. She didn't move away, and I brushed my thumb over her full lower lip. She shivered at my touch, and for a moment I let myself get lost in her wide-eyed stare.

"I know you feel it, too," I said, softly so as not to spook her. "The attraction between us. It's more than physical, even if that's all you see right now. That's okay. I can wait. I've waited all my life for you—I can wait a few more months. Or years, if that's how long it takes. But one day, you'll be my wife."

She stared at me for a long while, still with her mouth half-open. "I... You don't even know me. *I* don't know *you*."

I shrugged. "Doesn't matter."

"Of *course* it matters!" The outrage was back on her pretty face. "If you want a girl to marry you, then getting to know her is kind of the first step. Oh, and pro-tip: trying to force her to have your baby is not really a great selling point, either."

I released her chin with a regretful twinge. "I will get to know you, Evelyn. I will do anything I must to make you mine. But right now, I have to go see my other brothers. Will you come with me?"

"Oh." Some of the indignant huff seemed to deflate from her posture, as if she wasn't sure how to respond—

whether to my declaration that she would be mine or the invitation to come with me, I couldn't tell. Then she visibly steeled herself off and nodded "I'll come with you if you think that's a good idea. I'd like to get outside for a bit, but maybe they would rather not a complete stranger was there when you tell them this? Blaine didn't exactly seem thrilled."

"You saw the video—you are my proof, if I need it. They are... closer with my father than me or Blaine." And if I didn't bring her, they would undoubtedly show up at my doorstep the moment Blaine told them about her, anyway. And I'd rather they knew about her from me before they mentioned anything to my father. I didn't want him to hear about her without me in the room so I could see his reaction. He likely wouldn't care much, but I wasn't about to risk Evelyn's safety in case the malicious man who had ruled my life from the day I was born decided she didn't fit into his plans for the Family.

Silently, I walked over to retrieve Evelyn's coat. She let me help her shrug into it and didn't protest when I wound my arm around her midriff to support most of her weight. She might have been able to walk without limping too much now, but I didn't want the cuts on her feet to start bleeding again.

The thought of how badly hurt her soles had been after Leo's mistreatment made the monster rear its head and snarl. I pushed it down with the grim satisfaction of knowing that he'd had enough time to regret what he'd done to her before he drew his last breath.

No one was ever going to hurt her again. Evelyn was mine, and no one would ever take her away from me. Not even her.

## SEVENTEEN

### EVELYN

I spent the car ride to Marcus' brothers' place staring wide-eyed at him from the passenger seat. Either he didn't notice or he didn't mind, because not once did he return my gaze.

I'd had boyfriends before, but not a single relationship had lasted past the three-week mark, and certainly no one had ever declared that they were going to marry me before. And then, out of nowhere, the man I had stolen from claimed I would be his wife no matter what it took.

The baby was bad enough—but I had been able to make sense of that, somewhat. He wanted an heir and I had a womb—I could understand the business-like approach to it, even if I didn't particularly appreciate it.

But *this...?*

This wasn't about business, or repayment for what I did to him. This was... Despite myself, I felt my heart flutter in my chest as I recalled what he'd said. That we belonged together—that he'd waited all his life for me.

It was absurd, of course. There was no such thing as fate, no such thing as soulmates, and no happy ending for the girl who had fucked up her life beyond repair by getting involved with the mafia.

But there was still a tiny part of me that had yearned something fierce when he told me he would do whatever it took to marry me. No one had ever wanted me enough to say something like that, and no one but my mother had ever really shown that they cared enough about me to go out of their way for me.

He wasn't wrong when he said that I felt it too, though what "*it*" was, I wasn't entirely sure. I'd been drawn to him from the moment I first saw him, even with all his looming danger and darkness. I'd written it off as purely physical attraction, but deep down, I knew that wasn't it.

Deep down, I knew some stupid part of me longed for what he said to be true.

But I was too old to believe in fairy tales and happy endings, and whatever was between me and Marcus, it wasn't love. We didn't even know each other, for crying out loud!

I gritted my teeth against the inexplicable pang of longing.

What I needed was to not be involved with another crime family any longer than I had to. Getting out of this arrangement we had going as soon as this whole Brigs thing was solved was the pragmatic thing to do, and I was nothing if not pragmatic.

---

MARCUS' twin brothers shared a flat overlooking the Thames. It wasn't located in the same kind of luxurious and sleek apartment building that Marcus lived in, but a re-purposed old brick factory. Still, when Marcus let us into the flat with a pair of keys he produced from his pocket, it was quite obvious that it wasn't a place I'd ever be able to afford for myself.

The floors were polished hardwood and the view from the living room we stepped into was every bit as amazing as Marcus'.

"They won't mind that you just let yourself in?" I asked in a low tone as he let his gaze sweep over the room, likely searching for clues to the whereabouts of his brothers.

"No. Sit down while I get them." He walked toward the leather sofa in front of a giant flat screen TV, effectively dragging me along by the grip he had around my waist.

I obeyed, not bothering to argue that my feet really didn't hurt. I'd tried that on multiple occasions already, and it'd all fallen on deaf ears.

Marcus made sure I was comfortable on the couch before he turned around and stalked toward the hallway leading further into the flat. I heard a door open, followed by distinct moaning.

*Oh, God!* I flushed hotly when I realized what Marcus had undoubtedly just walked in on.

I couldn't hear what he said to interrupt them, but the moaning stopped and the female voice that followed shrilled through the apartment.

Shortly after, I heard the door close again and had a moment's worth of hoping we'd be leaving before whichever brother had just been disturbed had the chance to meet me, but that hope was crushed when the sound of another door being opened—followed by an indignant shout—echoed into the living room.

Shortly thereafter Marcus appeared around the corner again, looking as disinterested as if nothing out of the ordinary had happened.

"Should we be leaving?" I asked.

"No. They'll be out shortly." He arched an eyebrow at my attempt at getting up. "You stay seated. Your feet—"

"Yeah yeah," I sighed, falling back down on the cushion again. "My feet are delicate petals. You do realize this is highly inappropriate, right? We should really come back when they're not busy."

Marcus shrugged. Apparently, he wasn't the least bit fussed over walking in on his brothers having sex.

We didn't wait more than five minutes before the two doors further into the flat opened almost simultaneously, and two blonde girls stomped through to the living room and headed straight for the front door. If looks could kill, Marcus would have been stone cold dead.

The door slammed after them hard enough for the flat screen to shake.

"You're toeing the edge of losing your key, you wanker," an annoyed male voice sounded. I looked up just as a redheaded guy rounded the corner, an irritated expression plastered across his face. He was wearing nothing but a maroon pair of boxers that clashed spectacularly with his messy ginger hair.

His spitting image appeared behind him, wearing an identical scowl. I blinked at the double vision. Marcus had said they were twins, all right, but I'd never seen two people who looked more alike than these brothers—the only thing that set them apart was that the latecomer had on a pair of fluorescent orange shorts. They didn't look much like Marcus and Blaine, who I'd easily been able to tell were brothers, though the vast expanse of bare skin currently on display made it plenty obvious that they were still attractive men.

I did my best to not look anywhere below their shoulders as I struggled to get up from the couch once more, but Marcus planted a large hand on my shoulder and pressed me down without effort.

"Well, well, what do we have here?" Orange Boxers asked as his gray eyes zeroed in on me.

"Hi," I said, doing my best to not blush again at the

awkward encounter. "And sorry. I told him we should leave."

"Common sense is not our brother's strongest suit, love," Maroon said as he looked me up and down. "Which is why I gotta ask if he's kidnapped you, or you're here of your own free will?"

Out of the corner of my eye I saw Marcus' face turn dangerously dark. If the twins noticed, they ignored him.

"Er... free will," I offered, quirking an eyebrow at them. "Dare I ask?"

Orange shrugged and fell down on the couch next to me, spreading his arms across the back of it as if we were old friends. "You look an awful lot like our mother, and with that weird Oedipal complex our brother Blaine's got going on with his wife, you never know."

"Evelyn is my fiancée," Marcus growled, the warning clear in his voice. "You'll treat her with respect."

Maroon choked on a cough, and next to me, Orange turned his head to stare at me so fast I heard his neck pop.

Maroon recovered first. "Well, well, seems the Steel men have a type. Better watch out, or we might end up accidentally marrying the next curvy little redhead that crosses our paths, eh, Liam?" He shot me a disarming smile.

"Well, congratulations. I always assumed you'd end up abducting a bride, or something, so well done on landing a bird who's actually sticking around voluntarily," Orange said. He was still massaging his neck with one hand. "I'm kind of curious what made you two crazy kids hook up, though. Last I heard, our dear brother wasn't exactly seeing anyone."

I glanced at Marcus, unsure of how to explain our arrangement—especially now that he was adamant we'd end up getting married. The vaguely humorous note that he had, in fact, abducted me off the street wasn't lost on me, though.

"We're not here to discuss Evelyn," Marcus said. He gestured toward the armchair next to Orange—or Liam—at Maroon. "Sit down, Louis. This is serious."

Louis' amused smile faltered and he moved to the chair, seemingly not bothered that his brother was ordering him about in his own home.

"What is it, then?" Liam asked. He, too, had lost the note of humor from his voice. "Is it about Brigs?"

"No," Marcus said. His mouth was set in a grim line as he took a seat on the coffee table so he could face both the twins. Something about his posture made me think that it was harder for him to broach the subject with Louis and Liam than it had been with Blaine. "It's about Dad. And Jeremy."

I watched the twins as Marcus told them everything about the video he'd taken of their father ordering Jeremy's murder, what Blaine had told him about their other brother's arrest, and finally, what he and Blaine had discussed. Both their faces grew darker and darker, grief etching into their features until Marcus finished talking.

They both looked at each other then, and I got the sense that something passed between them—some sort of communication neither Marcus or I could interpret.

When they finally looked back, it was at me.

"How is she involved?"

"I'm... not," I croaked, blanching.

"Love, there is no way our dear brother would have involved his new fiancée in any of this if he'd had a choice. He might be mad as fuck, but he's not dumb. What's your role in this?" Liam said.

"Brigs hired her to steal the video from me," Marcus said. If he was worried about revealing this tidbit to the twins, he didn't show it. "She watched it. She's the one who made me talk to you and Blaine."

"Of course. You're the girl he called us about," Louis said. He shook his head and looked back at Marcus. "What happened? She decided to switch teams and Brigs had Leo torture her?"

"Yes."

Liam got up from his seat and rubbed his hands through his messy hair with a long sigh. "Of course you couldn't find your wife at a nightclub like a normal person."

"What is the plan, then? Once Brigs is taken care of, how the fuck are we supposed to take down our own father?" Louis said. "He's the most powerful man in the bloody country."

"I don't know," Marcus said, his tone surprisingly soft. "But we have to try."

"Yeah. We do," Liam said. He was leaning against the wall, and despite the anguish still plain on his face, there was a look of determination in his eyes when he glanced back at his twin. "I'm not losing any more brothers to him."

THE DARKNESS that radiated off Marcus was stronger than normal as he drove us back to his flat, but I found it didn't unsettle me like it had in the beginning. Somewhat to my confusion it just made me want to touch him, offer my support in some way. I didn't, though. Something about reaching out for him after his declaration that we somehow *belong together* made me hesitate. As if touching him would mean that I agreed.

Wanted to belong with him.

Sharp fear clenched in my stomach, and I frowned. I'd never thought of myself as the romantic type—I'd learned early on that men weren't to be trusted when my dad up and left my mother and me when I was still a kid, and working for Brigs had only confirmed it. Most of my marks had been married, and yet still they came willingly at the promise of sex with a stranger.

I'd never wanted to be part of a couple, so why did I care whether or not Marcus did?

When we got back to Marcus' flat it was past six in the evening, and I headed straight for the fridge as my stomach grumbled about having missed lunch. Before I could let my eyes roam over the fancy ingredients Marcus had stocked his fridge with, a large hand came down on my shoulder.

"Go sit down. I'll cook."

I craned my neck up to look at him. "Don't be silly— it's kind of my job. And besides, you've had a tough day. I'll try to whip up something slightly better than the pasta."

He didn't quite manage to hide the grimace that passed over his face at the mention of my failed pasta dish, and I couldn't help but feel just a tiny bit insulted.

"It wasn't *that* bad!"

Marcus didn't respond, and I huffed at his raised eyebrow.

"Fine, whatever. You play *MasterChef*, then. I'll watch CSI and wait on your culinary creations." I didn't quite stomp off to the sofa, though I did sit down on the couch with a demonstrative huff.

It didn't take long for mouthwatering scents to waft over to the lounge area, and when Marcus finally placed a plate with a large steak, buttered potatoes, and pan seared veggies in front of me, I didn't have it in me to stay insulted.

"Oh my God, this looks absolutely amazing," I said,

already grabbing knife and fork to dig in. The first bite was heaven.

"Mouth orgasm," I moaned around a big chunk of meat. "How are you such a good cook?" I scarfed down another bite, humming happily. "This is legit the best food I've ever tasted."

"I wanted to own a café, once," he said. He sat next to me on the couch with his own plate, but he managed it with quite a bit more grace than I. "Took some cooking classes, until my father found out."

"I guess it's not that easy to get out of the family busi-ness, in your situation," I said in between unladylike bites. Up until now, it had never dawned on me that he'd even want to. "When did you try?"

"When I was sixteen. I always used to help my mother in the kitchen. It took a few years after her death until I could go near one again."

He said it so calmly, with no hint of emotion, but the revelation still made my heart give an achy spasm of empathy.

"I'm so sorry. I didn't know you'd lost her," I said, finally looking up from my already half-devoured food.

He gave a shrug, but the stiffness of his shoulders told me he was just putting on a show. There was an old wound there.

"What happened? If... if you're okay talking about it."

"One of the Family's rivals got to her. She liked to go for evening walks around the neighborhood. I usually came with her. I didn't that night—it was the same night my father had some of the men teach me about guns for the first time. That's why they got to her—the men who were supposed to guard the neighborhood were securing the warehouse they used for target practice."

I didn't think about it this time—I just reached out and placed my hand on his knee, wanting somehow to ease the pain I could almost see behind his dark gaze. "It wasn't your fault. You know that, right? If you'd been there, you would have died too."

Marcus shrugged again, his sensitive lips twisting into a frown. "Maybe. Or maybe they would have been content with killing a Steel son rather than an innocent woman. She was very kind. Good. Not like the rest of us." He looked at me and his gaze turned softer. "You remind me of her."

I couldn't help the hot flush I felt spread to my cheeks. "I'm not really all that kind. Or good. I worked for Brigs for a year and a half—I don't think anyone who's done what I have can be classed as *good*."

He put his fork down and placed his now free hand on top of mine. The heat from it flowed up my arm with a pleasant buzz. "What have you done?"

There was no judgment in his tone, nor unease. Only his usual calmness. The lingering softness in his eyes as he looked at me made all the guilt I'd spent so long suppressing come bubbling to the surface.

"I'm the reason people got hurt. A lot of people. I

lured them into the trap, and I knew what would happen to them once they walked into it. I never stayed once Leo and his men had their hands on them, but I knew." I was too ashamed to keep eye contact and looked down to where our hands were joined. How ironic that I felt such intense shame over the crimes I'd facilitated in front of a mafia son. But that soft look in his eyes, hearing him compare me to his dead mother whom he obviously thought the world of... it made me feel like such a fraud. Even though he, of all people, should have known what kind of work I'd done.

"I never slept with any of them." I don't know what possessed me to say that, but it somehow felt important that he knew he was the only one I'd had sex with for the job. As if that somehow would make me purer.

"Even if you did, it wouldn't change what you are deep down," he rumbled, his hand moving to nudge my chin up. "You put your own life on the line for mine. You protected me."

And there it was. I opened my mouth to deny it, to tell him that wasn't what happened, but the words died on my lips. That was exactly what had happened. I'd wanted to protect him, the man I was meant to seduce so Brigs could have taken him and his family down. But when it came down to it, I couldn't. And I had put my own life on the line to protect him.

"Why did you work for him?" he asked.

I shrugged. "I was stupid and borrowed money off him

that I couldn't pay back. It was that job or... well, I'm sure you know what happens to people who don't pay back a loan to a guy like Brigs."

"What did you need the money for?"

I bit my lip, thinking back to when the doctor had first told me that there was nothing more they could do for my mother. That she was going to slip further and further away from me until she was nothing but a shell of the woman she'd once been. "My mum has Alzheimer's. There is a private nursing home up in Highgate that specializes in the care of people with dementia and Alzheimer's, and I couldn't... I couldn't face the thought that I couldn't get her the best care possible. She's always looked after me, and since my dad left, it's always been her and me against the world. I couldn't live with myself if I let her down when she needed me the most. But the bank wouldn't lend me any money—apparently, being a waitress doesn't inspire great financial trust. So I found Brigs." I glanced up at him. "That's what I spent the money that was missing from what I stole from you on, too. I paid one of the nurses to look after her for me, since I thought I'd have to flee the country."

The expression on Marcus' face was as gentle as I'd ever seen it. It made me falter, my voice dying as his gray eyes connected with mine. "*Anything for the Family*. It's the Steel motto, but you put us all to shame, Evelyn. You've risked everything to take care of your mother. It doesn't make you a bad person. It makes you strong."

"I don't feel strong," I admitted, my voice quavering a little as I took in the admiration in his gaze. It felt undeserved, and yet everything inside of me hungered for more the longer our eyes connected. I looked down to our hands again. "I've been scared for what feels like years. It feels like the only thing that's kept me going is that I'm more scared of not doing right by my mum than I am of what I've seen and done."

Marcus' hand constricted slightly around mine, and when he spoke this time, there was a hint of steel in his voice. "You don't have to be scared anymore. I'm here now —and I will take care of both you and your mother. I promise."

# EIGHTEEN

## EVELYN

Marcus didn't join me in bed that night, and when I woke up the next morning, I was still alone.

Somewhat odd behavior, really, for a guy who proclaimed to want to impregnate me. If I'd ever been open to the idea of having his baby, it had been after he told me he would take care of not only me, but also my mother. Something about the sincerity in his eyes resonated with that same aspect of myself that had been so drawn to him from the very first time we met, and I had allowed myself to imagine just what it'd be like to be a happy little family unit.

But Marcus hadn't followed me to bed, and in the clarity of daylight, I was pretty thankful I hadn't indulged in a round of unprotected sex. As much as he might mean it *right now*, no one could say how long that would last—

and I didn't need to add a baby to my problems once he and I inevitably went our separate ways.

Even if it had felt good to believe for just a few moments.

I got out of bed, ruthlessly pushing down any lingering emotions inspired by our candid talk last night, and trotted to the bathroom to get ready for the day.

I found Marcus at the dining table with a bowl of half-eaten yogurt pushed to the side and his focus solely on the laptop in front of him.

"Morning," I offered as I passed by on my way to the fridge.

He only grunted in return, but when I joined him at the table a few minutes later with my freshly toasted cream-cheese bagel, he finally lifted his eyes from the screen.

There were a hint of dark circles under his eyes, and I wondered if he had even slept at all last night.

"Did you not make it to bed?" I asked before sinking my teeth into the bagel. "Did one of your brothers get in touch with a plan? Or is it about Brigs?"

"No." He closed the laptop and looked at me with an expression I couldn't quite decipher. "When you've finished your breakfast, I'd like us to go visit your mother."

I coughed, choking on my mouthful of food. "Why?"

"I thought you might like to see her."

"Of course I would, but I..." I hadn't thought I would ever get to again. An odd mix of relief, excitement, and worry circulated in my chest, making it feel tight. "I don't want Brigs to know about her. Does he know where you live? Is there a chance he'd have us followed?"

Marcus shrugged. "If he does, it won't help him any. I've sent men up to guard her nursing home—the building will be protected at all times."

I blinked, repeatedly, as warmth and confusion spread through my body. "I... how do you know which nursing home she's at?"

"There's only one nursing home in Highgate that specializes in dementia and Alzheimer's." He said it matter-of-factly, as if stationing criminal *guards* around a nursing home was a perfectly normal thing to do.

"Oh." I stared at him for several long moments while my brain slowly processed the one burning question his revelation left me with. "Why are you doing this?"

"My father might have forgotten what our motto used to be, but I haven't. She is your family, and that makes her mine. I told you—I will protect both of you. At any cost."

SUSIE WASN'T on the front desk when Marcus and I passed through the reception, but the nurse there recognized me and let us through with a courteous nod—and a wary look at Marcus' large figure.

"Stay behind me, okay?" I said to him as we paused outside my mother's door. "She gets confused easily, and...

well, you're kind of scary. So please don't take offense if I ask you to wait outside, okay?"

Marcus gave a short nod, seemingly not too offended by that, nor by being called scary. I offered him a smile as thanks and knocked once on the door before opening it.

"Mum? It's me. Evelyn. I brought a visitor. Is that okay?"

She was sitting by the window as she usually did, but turned toward the door at the sound of my voice. My heart gave a spasm of joy when a smile of recognition spread across her face.

"Evelyn. I didn't expect to see you today, my love. It isn't Tuesday, is it?"

"No, it's not, Mum." I walked over and hugged her tightly, breathing in her scent in greedy gulps. Her lucid days were getting fewer and farther between, and I was overwhelmed with a sudden rush of gratitude toward Marcus for bringing me here today. "I just missed you and wanted to stop by and say hi."

"Don't you be missing out on your life to come check up on me, child," she said, giving my shoulders a squeeze with surprising strength. "The nurses here take excellent care of me."

"I'm not missing out on anything." Reluctantly, I let go of her when she pulled back, but her focus shifted behind me and her eyebrows crept up.

"And who is this young man you've brought along to meet your old mother?" Her eyes sparkled mischievously. "The future father of my grandchildren, perhaps?"

"Mum!" I protested, already sensing the heat gathering in my cheeks. "You can't just harass any guy you see for grandchildren."

"I am Marcus Steel, Mrs. Embry," Marcus said, his rumbling voice carrying easily across the room, though it sounded softer than usual. "It's a pleasure to meet you. Evelyn speaks of you very fondly."

"She's a good girl," my mum agreed, completely ignoring my flustered presence. "Come here, young man. Let me get a better look at you."

He obeyed, and even knelt down next to her chair when she motioned for him to do so.

Without shame, my mother placed both her hands on each side of his face. "And such a handsome one, too. Do you treat my little girl right? If she's brought you to see me, she must be very keen on you. Do you feel the same about her?"

"*Mum!*" I hissed, my cheeks now in full flame. I'd forgotten how completely straightforward she could be.

Marcus put his hands over my mum's, engulfing them completely. "I will take care of Evelyn until the day I die."

The corners of my mum's eyes crinkled when she gave him a sweet smile. "Good. It's hard for her to trust—she never did get over her dad leaving, the poor child. But I think you might just be the man to change that, won't you?"

His face, normally so serious and dark, became light and gentle when his mouth pulled up to reciprocate her smile. "Yes."

My mum finally released his face and turned to the window again. "Come sit with me. I would like to get to know my future son-in-law."

I stood back and watched. It was as if I looking through a kaleidoscope into an alternate dimension, where my mother and the man who had taken me in discussed the birds outside my mum's window, recipes for raspberry jam, and the importance of a strong father figure when it came to child rearing as if they had known each other for years. All the while completely ignoring me.

It was an odd sensation, looking at the only two people in my life who had ever taken care of me and knowing that this perfect slice of life would never truly be mine. That it was a fleeting moment in time showcasing what might have been, if life had turned out differently.

And yet, even as my heart clenched with longing for what I could never have, I was still infinitely grateful that I had been given this one moment where everything was just perfect. It was more than I'd thought I could hope for since I had to give up everything to work for Brigs.

When it was time to leave, my mum pulled Marcus into a hug before she turned to me for the first time since greeting me. "Come say goodbye, Evelyn."

I walked over and into her arms, closing my eyes to

soak in the warmth when she closed them around me. It felt as good as it had when I was a kid.

"You marry that man, love," she said softly into my ear. "He has a good heart, behind all that pain he's carrying. He will take care of you when I'm gone."

"You're not going anywhere, Mum," I choked into her hair. "Not now, not ever."

"Shh, child. I know my mind is slipping away, and it's going to do you no good to pretend like it isn't. Someday soon it will be completely gone, and when that happens, I want you to be with someone who will treasure you and make you as happy as you've made me since the day I gave birth to you. He loves you, it's plain to see the way he looks at you when he thinks you're not watching. And if you are brave enough to open yourself up to him, I think you'll find love in your heart for him, too. I know you, my daughter. Don't let fear stand in the way of your own happiness."

"It's not that simple," I whispered, doing my best to stem the tears that prickled my eyes. "We're not together that way. There are... reasons."

"There are always reasons, Evelyn." She pulled back from our embrace and cupped my face for a short moment, brushing away the single tear that had escaped my attempt at holding my emotions back. "And it's never simple. I can tell he's not an uncomplicated man, he has pain and darkness. But if he is as devoted to you as I believe, you let him in and don't ever let go. Don't throw away your chance at happiness because your father was an idiot."

"I've missed you, Mum," I said, reaching out to squeeze her hand one last time before I straightened up.

She smiled that gentle smile of hers that had brought me through every painful moment after my dad left. "I love you, Evelyn. Always. Now, go—you have a good man waiting for you, love. And I will be here again next week."

But she wouldn't. We both knew that—it had been over a month since the last time she had been even remotely this clear-headed. I bent to kiss her cheek, managing to keep myself together for her sake. Crying would only make her feel bad, and that was the last thing I wanted on one of her fleetingly few good days.

"I love you too, Mum. See you next week."

Marcus was waiting for me outside the door, having given us some privacy to say goodbye. He didn't say anything when he saw me brush a few stray tears away, but he put his arm around my shoulders as we walked down the hallway toward the nursing home's exit. His warmth and the strength of his body against mine felt good—it steeled me against the onslaught of emotion warring in my own body, keeping me up like a life jacket in a tumultuous sea.

"She is a lovely woman," he said when we exited the building and paused in front of the visitors' parking lot where he'd parked his Porsche.

"Yeah. She's everything to me." I offered him a weak smile. "She was very fond of you."

"And I her." He touched a hand to my chin, lifting my gaze to his. The fondness in his gray eyes made my heart flutter in response. "I see where you get your kindness from."

I scoffed. "I am nothing like her. She is so sweet and so generous—she could never hurt anyone, would never let a man like Brigs ruin her sense of right and wrong."

"I think you might be surprised what she would do to keep the ones she loves safe. Just like you did for her—just like I will for you both." And then he dipped his head and pressed his lips to mine.

The kiss was gentle, and yet it made my heart hammer behind my ribs and my breath whoosh out in small gasps when he broke it off much too soon.

I stared up at him, my mother's words replaying in my mind as I saw the gentleness in his gaze as he looked at me.

Was there any way we could make this work? He was still part of a crime family, still everything I'd promised myself I would stay far, far away from the moment I was free from Brigs. His world was danger and darkness at every turn.

And if I let myself fall for the promise of love—of baring my soul to him and having his in return—and he then ended up pushing me away... I wouldn't survive it. This time, my mother wouldn't be there to pick up the pieces, and I knew that if I opened my heart to Marcus and he left me I would never be whole again.

But was I truly whole now? When everything in me yearned for that sweet pull between us and all I wanted was to give in?

"Can we go for a short walk? Before we drive back?" I asked, finally making a decision. It made my stomach churn with anxiety, but also elation.

"If you wish," he said. Once again he wrapped an arm around my shoulders, and once again the sensation of security set in.

I saw him nodding at a man standing discreetly off to the side of the entrance to the nursing home and was momentarily distracted from my nervousness. "Is that one of the guards you talked about?" I asked, keeping my voice low so as not to attract attention.

Marcus nodded as he led me across the street toward a small park we'd passed on the way here.

"Thank you," I said as we walked the couple of blocks along the quiet road. "For making sure she is safe. And for taking me here today. She doesn't have many good days anymore."

"I am glad you let me meet her," he said. "I wish I could have introduced you to my mother, as well. I think you would have liked her."

"Would she have liked me?" I asked, suddenly feeling weirdly nervous if I would have been what his mother wanted for him.

"Yes," he said, and I could hear a rare smile in his voice even without looking up at him to confirm. "She would have liked you very much."

"And your brothers? You think they... approve?" I thought back to the surprise in all three men's faces when Marcus had declared me his fiancée, and frowned when I thought about the twins' comments about the probability of him abducting a bride.

He shrugged. "I think so. If not, they will."

"You just know that, huh?"

"Yes." He didn't elaborate, and I didn't want to push. Instead I focused on the cool winter air and the smell of soil as we entered the park through the wrought iron gates. Marcus released my shoulders and instead offered his arm, and I rested my hand on it as we slowly strolled along the path.

It was a typical English winter, cold but not freezing, and the ground was wet from last night's rain. As the bushes and trees closed around us, I could almost ignore the sounds of cars coming from the street outside the park —could almost pretend like it was just me and Marcus in all the world.

"Marcus, I... was wondering..." *Here goes nothing.* "If we... if we did end up together, how would it work? With your dad and your job and... I don't want to be involved with the mafia, and that's your life. Your family."

He glanced down at me, but the sky was starting to

darken and I couldn't make out the expression in his eyes. "You won't be involved. Mira isn't."

"That's not how it works for me," I said softly. "I'll know what you do every day when you leave. I'll know that you hurt people. That you *kill*. I... I've had enough of that to last a lifetime. I don't want any more violence in my life, or fear that someone like Brigs might try to hurt us because of what you do."

"What do you want?" he asked.

I sighed. "Peace. I've done so many horrible things while working for Brigs. I just want peace. I want to plant my own veggie patch and sell produce at farmer's markets and make raspberry jam with you. To wake up in the morning and not wonder if my husband has killed someone while I slept, and how long their family will mourn." It wasn't until I stopped talking I realized I'd said I wanted it—with him.

Marcus stopped on the path, and I stopped with him, looking up at him and knowing that I was hoping for the impossible. He was a mafia son, he was born into the violence I was so desperate to escape. But then his hand brushed away a stray lock of hair that had stuck to my cheek, and a reflection of the city lights finally let me see his eyes. There was as much tenderness in them as there was in his touch, and my heart fluttered with renewed hope.

"Evelyn—"

His voice cut out as a dark-clad figure stepped out

from behind the bushes just a few yards further down the path, and even before I'd fully realized what was going on, Marcus let out a furious roar and leapt forward, pushing me behind him.

A deafening gunshot rang through the air and Marcus' forward momentum came to an abrupt halt. He dropped to the ground on his knees with a low groan, clutching at his side. And I screamed.

The man still holding a gun slowly turned from Marcus, his outstretched arm now pointing at me.

Time froze as I stared at the barrel. There was nothing I could do to escape it, nowhere I could hide. My heart pounded in my chest and all I could think about was that I didn't want to die.

The gunman's trigger finger flexed, but the next shot that rang through the park wasn't his. Marcus had managed to pull a weapon from inside his long wool coat and fired it the second before our attacker, hitting him in the leg.

The man bellowed, his finger slipping on the trigger as yet another shot fired—this time from his gun. But it didn't hit me. The blast from Marcus' gun managed to divert his focus, and his bullet fired off to the side and into Marcus' chest.

This time, the sound that escaped Marcus' lips was only a soft gasp as he collapsed on the ground, no longer moving.

A pool of red bloomed on the front of his coat.

## NINETEEN

EVELYN

"Marcus! No, no, *no!*" I cried as I threw myself by his side, only faintly aware that our attacker had given up on finishing the job and instead limped further into the park as fast as he could. It was a good thing too, because all I cared about then and there was Marcus. I fumbled for my phone and called 999 with shaky fingers, all the while pressing my left hand against the wound through his woolen coat.

"*Emergency central, which department do you need?*" an operator asked.

"I need an ambulance." It was only when I spoke that I noticed I was crying. My voice was rough and broken, but thankfully the woman understood me. She put me through to medical emergencies, and I managed to gasp out what had happened and where we were. The man on the other end told me to keep pressure on Marcus' wound and he stayed on the line while I babbled pleas at Marcus to wake up.

When the ambulance finally came I was numb with fear and grief, but after staring at Marcus' unmoving figure and feeling his blood seep out between my fingers, at least I knew one thing with absolute and frightening clarity.

I loved him.

I loved him, and there was no point in denying it, no point in pretending like the obstacles between us were impossible to climb, because in the end, it didn't matter whether or not I willingly gave my heart to him. He already owned it, and as I climbed in the back of the ambulance after his still form strapped to a gurney, I knew the only thing I had earned from hesitating was knowing that he might die unaware that I would give anything to be his.

"MRS. STEEL?"

I looked up from my still bloody hands. I hadn't had the presence of mind to wash them while I waited for forty-five minutes as the hospital staff operated on Marcus.

It was one of the doctors I'd seen disappear in behind the doors alongside his gurney.

My heart throbbed as I got to my feet. I was unsure if

standing up right now was the smartest thing to do.

"He's going to be fine. The bullet in his chest missed his heart and went straight through, and we got the other one out of his side without complications." The doctor smiled at me as I stared uncomprehendingly at his face.

"He's okay?" I croaked, wanting to make sure I'd heard right.

"Yes. He's a tough one. He woke up while I was still stitching him up and threatened one of the nurses when she tried to give him more morphine. He's asking for you." He put a hand on my shoulder. "He's in recovery now, but I think you best come along so he doesn't attempt to get out of bed and come looking for you. You'll be doing him a big favor if you convince him to settle down and rest."

Relief so powerful it nearly knocked my legs out from underneath me flooded through my body. He was okay. He wasn't going to die.

"Thank you," I said, once more choking on a flood of tears I could do nothing to stem. "Thank you so, so much."

"Just doing my job," the doctor said as he led me through the double doors. "But be prepared. The police will have questions for the both of you. Especially since they found a gun on your husband, as well."

I nodded, not really capable of caring too much about that, because just then he opened the door into a single room and my eyes locked on Marcus.

He was propped up in a hospital bed with white bandages around his chest and torso, but the look on his face was not what you'd expect from a man who had just taken two bullets. He looked *furious,* and the poor nurse by his bedside looked like she was about to tear up.

"Please, sir, you really need to let me put a drip in," she said, her voice quavering as she held out a needle.

But instead of rebutting her, Marcus' attention snapped to the door as I entered alongside the doctor— and his expression changed completely. Relief washed over his handsome features and the rage that had clearly been bubbling just underneath the surface vanished like snow on a hot summer's day.

"*Evelyn!* Are you hurt?"

I laughed, which came out as a sad hiccup thanks to the ample amounts of snot and tears still clogging up my sinuses. "I'm fine. I'm not the one who got in the way of a loaded gun, remember?" I walked over to his side, the nurse happily stepping back to let me take my place. "I thought..."

"Let's give them some space, Edwina," the doctor said from the door. "We can come back in a little while and see if Mr. Steel has calmed down a bit."

I didn't hear the nurse's response, but from the way the door shut seconds later, I took it she had no problem with that suggestion.

"Are you giving the staff a hard time?" I asked, eying the abandoned IV next to his bed. "They're only trying to help."

"They wouldn't let me get up and look for you," he

said, a frown making itself known between his eyebrows. "I didn't know if you'd been hurt."

"No, you saved me," I said quietly, letting my hand find his. "He was going to shoot me too, but you diverted the bullet when you shot him. I thought he'd killed you."

"It takes more than Brigs' scum to take me down," he said, and I couldn't hold back a small laugh.

"I hadn't pegged you for being one of those bone-headed guys who thinks being taken down by a bullet is a sign of weakness."

He arched an eyebrow at my mocking, and my laughter died down as the thoughts I'd had while I sat by his lifeless body came rushing back. But saying it out loud now, while he was looking at me proved harder than I'd anticipated.

"Marcus, I..."

"I love you, Evelyn," he said softly, cutting me off before I could force myself to continue. "I understand if you cannot return my feelings. I know I am... not someone a good woman could envision her future with. But from the first time I saw you, I knew I was meant to love you, and I can't do anything to change that. All I ask is that you let me be around you. Let me provide for you and ensure you're safe. I don't need anything else."

"I love you too." It flowed out between my lips more easily than I could ever have imagined.

Marcus stared at me for a couple of seconds, and then realization seemed to dawn on his face. A broad smile that lit up his eyes spread across his lips and radiated into me like the warmth of the sunrise after a long winter's night. He pushed himself up and reached out for me, clasping both hands around my waist and pulling me closer, even as a pained groan escaped his lips as he did.

"Be careful!" I cried as he pressed me in tight against his bandaged chest, but Marcus didn't pay me nor his injuries any mind. He clasped the back of my head, and then closed his mouth over mine in a desperate kiss.

I gasped against his lips, overwhelmed by the passion and urgency, but when he moaned *"Evelyn"* into my mouth so softly it sounded like a prayer, I lost the will to fight it.

When the doctor walked in some time later, I was laying halfway across his lap, still so swept up in our kiss that I didn't notice we were no longer alone.

I jolted in Marcus' grasp and looked over my shoulder as the doctor cleared his throat, a hot flush already spreading in my cheeks.

"While it's nice to see my patient's in good spirits, perhaps it would be best to wait on any *gymnastic* activities until those wounds have had a chance to heal, hmm?"

Marcus's lip curled up in a silent snarl, but thankfully he didn't voice his displeasure at being interrupted when I shot him an admonishing glare.

"Sorry, doctor."

"Are you ready for your IV now, Mr. Steel?" the

doctor asked, both eyebrows raised at Marcus. "You scared my nurse so bad she refused to try again."

Marcus opened his mouth, and from the irritated expression on his face it was obvious he was going to refuse it.

"He's ready," I cut in, sending him a warning look.

"I don't need—"

I put my hand across his mouth, silencing him. "You need to rest and heal, and medicine will help with that. You let the man do his job—and no more barking at the nurses, either."

Marcus shot me a baleful look, but he let the doctor put the needle in his hand and hook up the drip. When we were once again alone in the room, he relaxed against the pillows propping him up. From the drowsy look in his eyes, it was obvious they'd put some pretty hefty drugs in his bag.

"We need to let my family know. They can intervene with the police," he said, his words a little slurred.

I smiled at his attempt at keeping his eyes open. "I'll take care of it. You just rest and get better, okay?"

"Mm," he grunted, finally losing the battle to the drugs as his eyelids closed.

I thought he had drifted off, but before I could get up from the side of his bed, he mumbled, "Evelyn?"

"Yeah?"

"The doctor called you my wife."

Oh. Right. That.

"I figured they'd let me stay if they thought we were married."

A small smile curled his lips, but he didn't respond. A few moments later, his breathing turned deep and slow.

I took in Marcus as he slept. Marcus, who had just declared his love for me. I had no idea how we were going to make it, with Brigs and his father looming in the background, but I knew I wanted to more than anything else. Even though the thought that he might change his mind and leave me still scared me stiff.

I pushed away  the pang of panic that unwelcome thought brought on and fished out my phone. Now was not the time to angst about my childhood trauma.

I sent Blaine a text explaining what had happened and where we were, and then curled up in the chair next to Marcus' bed to wait.

Blaine arrived twenty minutes later.

"You okay?" was the first thing he asked when he pushed in through the door, his eyes quickly scanning over his sleeping brother before they returned to me.

"Yeah, I wasn't hurt. Marcus got in between me and the man who attacked us." I unfolded myself from the chair, stretching tight muscles. The evening's events were starting to set in, and I wanted to just curl up next to Marcus and sleep more than anything. But I couldn't. He'd protected me in the park, and it was my turn to take care of him now. "The hospital has notified the police about what happened, and also that Marcus had a gun on him."

Blaine waved a hand. "It's taken care of. They won't be asking you any questions."

"Is it really that easy?" I said, frowning despite how the news should have made me happy rather than upset. "You have the right connections and the law no longer applies?"

"That's how it is in our world, sweetheart. And since you're engaged to a Steel, you better get used to it," Blaine said. "Especially now—Brigs attacked one of us openly and publicly. It's going to be all-out war from here on out, and paying off the police to keep their noses clear of it is not even going to register on the radar when all is said and done. It's not pretty, I know, but it's what you signed up for when you fell in love with my brother."

I swallowed thickly as I looked down at Marcus' still face. Blaine was right, of course. I'd known that all along. I couldn't have Marcus without also taking on the underworld he lived in.

But I knew I didn't have a choice anymore. I loved him too much to let go.

It took three days before the doctor would let me leave the hospital.

Of course, I could have ignored him and left when I woke up from my morphine haze the morning after being admitted, but Evelyn was having none of it. She insisted I stay in bed and let the hospital staff pump me full of drugs, and she was being pretty fucking stubborn about it.

So instead of getting up and getting even with Brigs for his attempt at my life, I'd spent nearly half a week in bed being coddled like a child. But when I tried to protest, she just looked at me with a stern expression in those beautiful eyes of hers, and everything in me sang with pure joy.

She *loved* me.

She loved me, and I knew I had finally found peace. I should have been fighting tooth and nail to keep the monster at bay after being taken down by an enemy, but it hadn't so much as reared its head. And it was because of *her*. Because of Evelyn.

I was home now, with her. My love. And for the first time in my life, I wasn't shrouded in darkness. There was light. Despite everything with Brigs, despite everything with my father—there was light.

I hugged her tight against my side, ignoring the twinge from my wounds as I once more made sure she was truly there—that I hadn't hallucinated the last three days.

"Careful!" Evelyn protested. "You'll hurt yourself, and don't think I'm not going to march you straight back in there for a full week if you pull your stitches!"

I smiled as I looked down at her messy ginger hair. The muscles in my face still hurt a little from the unaccustomed gesture—I'd smiled more in the past three days than I had since I was a child.

"Yes, ma'am."

She looked up at me and returned my smile, some of the sternness on her face softening. "You're way too happy for someone who's nursing two gunshot wounds, you know that, right?"

I bent to kiss her, enjoying the way her breath caught as much as the sweet sensation of her mouth under mine. I could have loved her without ever knowing what it was like to have my feelings reciprocated. That she loved me, too... nothing could ever compare.

"Mr. Steel?" a vaguely familiar voice called out. I

broke from the kiss and narrowed my eyes over Evelyn's head. I recognized the man as one of Blaine's men and the tension in my body eased some. My family had kept the hospital under highest watch while I'd been recuperating.

"Yes?"

"If you're ready, I've got a car waiting. Your father has requested you be taken directly to his house. Your brothers are there too, along with Blaine's wife and child."

I heaved a deep breath. As much as I didn't want to bring Evelyn anywhere near my father, I knew it was inevitable. With Brigs openly having me shot down, we had to circle the wagons—which meant convening at one location, where everyone could more easily be protected. At least I knew that, if Blaine had brought Mira and Aidan there, he was damn sure it was safe.

I glanced down at Evelyn and saw a worried frown marring her pretty face. "I'll make sure you're safe, always."

She looked up at me and managed a small smile. "I know. I trust you."

No one had ever trusted me before. Not fully. I knew my brothers trusted me to have their backs and that I would never screw them over, but it was different with Evelyn. She trusted me to protect her, to keep her safe and happy. She wasn't scared of me, like everyone else was. She'd seen the monster and still she trusted me. Loved me.

There was nothing I wouldn't do to keep her safe.

---

EVELYN HELD her head high as we walked through my father's mansion-like house, but I could tell from the strength she'd latched onto my arm with that she was nervous.

Not that I could blame her—even the building itself was imposing with its dark, wooden panels and high ceilings, but echoes of mostly male voices and running feet rang through the house from all corners. It was packed with our men, and she'd made it plenty clear that she wanted nothing more to do with the mafia if she got a say in the matter.

I led her through a couple of rooms past the entrance halls, toward the drawing room on the ground floor my father usually used for meetings, intent on getting Evelyn introduced as swiftly as possible.

He was seated behind the large desk, the twins and Blaine standing around it, and they were obviously in the middle of a discussion that broke off the moment we entered.

His steely eyes narrowed, even as one of the twins offered us both a welcoming smile.

"You're up! Glad you have decided to stop lazing about and lend a hand, brother," the redhead said, winking at Evelyn. "Hello again, love."

"Dad, I want you to meet Evelyn Embry. My fiancée,"

I said as we stopped in front of the desk, deciding to face the potential problem head on.

His cool eyes flickered across Evelyn. It made my heart swell with pride that she didn't shrink under his gaze—I knew strong men who practically shriveled up under less scrutiny than what she was currently receiving.

"Fiancée? And why have I heard nothing of this *fiancée* before now?" His gaze was back on me, but his tone made my three brothers suppress a cringe. It was obvious he wasn't happy with them for not mentioning Evelyn, either.

"It's new. I was going to introduce her to you the day I got shot," I lied smoothly, returning his gaze without blinking. Somehow, having Evelyn by my side made me feel stronger than I ever had when I faced the man who had ruled my life so brutally from the day I was born. "She stayed at the hospital with me—if you'd come to see me, you would have met then."

My father scowled. "A king can't leave his castle in the middle of a war. Even if his blood has fallen. I am, however, glad to see you are recovering well. And as for the girl... you are not married yet. She is not family."

"Where I go, she goes."

He arched an eyebrow at me and continued as if he hadn't heard me. "She can stay with Blaine's wife—safe, but out of the way."

It was a better deal than I had hoped for, so I nodded my

agreement. Evelyn would be safe and sound, if a little bored, until we had Brigs beat, and then I could take her back home. Thankfully, my father seemed only mildly irritated at my timing and otherwise completely uninterested in my choice of bride. I should count myself lucky—not fight down a small jab of pain that he was so uninterested in my happiness.

He had murdered Jeremy and put Isaac in jail. That he had little interest in me apart from the power my strength could provide him wasn't a surprise. But it still hurt.

"Blaine, take them to your wife's room. And after, you can show Marcus the little trump card we have in the basement."

Trump card? I lifted a brow at my older brother, but Blaine just turned around, heading out of the drawing room with a nod at Evelyn.

We both followed him in silence, my mind racing over what—or who—he could possibly be keeping in the basement. There was a soundproof room down there, with concrete floors and walls, and more than one unlucky sod had spent some unwilling time in it over the years. Did we have a hostage?

I glanced down at Evelyn. As much of an advantage a high-ranking hostage would be against Brigs, I'd rather she never learned about it. I was pretty sure keeping people prisoner was the exact sort of thing she didn't want any involvement with.

Blaine's right-hand man, Rob, stood leaned outside a

door on the second floor. He looked up from the process of cleaning his nails with his hunting knife and gave Blaine and I a nod when we walked down the hallway.

"Rob, this is Evelyn. I need you to guard her as well as you do Mira, understood?" Blaine said, looking back at the ginger girl by my side. "Any harm comes to her, you'll be dealing with my brother."

Rob didn't try to hide his grimace as his eyes flicked from Evelyn to me. "Got it."

"Evelyn, this is Rob—my right-hand man. He's a solid bloke. Don't hesitate to ask him for anything you need, yeah?" Blaine said.

She nodded, though I could tell from her arched brow that she likely had a few comments about this whole arrangement she was biting back.

I touched her cheek gently, capturing her attention. "I'll be back soon."

"*You* should be the one resting up in a room," she said with a frown. "You just got out of the hospital. I don't want you running around and getting yourself into any more trouble."

I ignored the amused flicker on both Rob's and Blaine's faces at Evelyn's bossy tone. "I'll be fine. I promise." I planted a quick peck on her lips and couldn't hold back a smile when she still looked rather unhappy as I pulled away. It was an entirely new experience that someone cared this much about my well-being.

"Ah, young love. Come on, brother, before your lovely

lady decides to shackle you to the wall. We have business to attend to." Blaine's tone was amused, but Evelyn flushed with obvious embarrassment at his comment. I glared at him, but if he noticed, he ignored me.

I gave Evelyn's hand a small squeeze, a reminder of my promise to return shortly, and then left her in Rob's care. As much as I'd rather stay with her and ensure her safety myself, I knew she would be as safe as possible with the man who was also responsible for Mira's security. And I had a war to fight. I'd been out for far too long, and despite everything, I wasn't about to leave my family alone to fight off our enemy.

Blaine led me down the stairs again and into the basement. It covered the full expanse of the house, and we made our way through our father's extensive wine cellar before we came to the closed metal door where both the twins were waiting for us.

"We caught a rat," Liam said, but the smile on his face held little joy. I knew neither of my younger brothers enjoyed the violent aspects of our job, preferring to handle the more above-board aspects of the business. But war was war, and no one was going to get out of this without getting their hands dirty.

"Brigs' right-hand man. Well, after Leo," Louis continued. "He's been stewing down here for the better part of twenty-four hours, so I do believe he might be ready to talk soon."

"Dad expects some information before dinner," Blaine

said. His mouth had a grim set, and it dawned on me that he didn't want to do what was necessary either.

"You brought me to torture him," I said. It wasn't a question.

"Well, he *did* shoot you," Liam said. "You usually don't take that kind of thing very well, but by all means, if you want to have a cozy chat instead... it would certainly make clean-up less sticky than usual."

A hot rush of anger washed through my body, setting off the so familiar tingle in my spine. "*He* is the one?" The one who tried to shoot Evelyn. *Hurt* her. My hands flexed with the need to *maim,* and I took a step forward toward the door, nearly giving in to the darkness swarming in from all sides.

I don't know where the tiny voice at the back of my mind came from, but it stopped me dead in my tracks as a single question rung in my head like a bell: *What would Evelyn say if she knew what I was about to do?*

Unexpected nausea pushed the descending darkness aside. I shook my head to clear it.

"We'll *talk* with him," I said, giving all three of my brothers a hard stare before I pushed through the door.

I didn't recognize the man who sat tied to a chair in the middle of the room, since his face had been hidden when he attacked us in the park, but he had a bandage wrapped around his leg in the exact spot I'd shot him to take his aim off Evelyn.

Again, the darkness pushed up to battle against my

self-control. This man had tried to *shoot* the woman I was meant to protect. My love. He didn't deserve to live.

But Evelyn hated violence. Had nearly refused a life with me because of the brutality in my world.

"You may remember our brother, Marcus," Louis said as he closed the door behind us. "Recently out of the hospital after you gunned him down. Not your biggest fan."

My attacker fidgeted in his ropes, his eyes roaming over my face. "The crazy one."

"Real smart move, aggravating him then, isn't it?" Liam said, rolling his eyes. "How about this—you tell us everything we want to know about Brigs and his plans, and we let you live. You're not going to get a better offer if our father has to come down here and speak to you himself, I can tell you that much."

The man in the chair narrowed his eyes. "Yeah? How about this, then: you untie me and let me go, tell your daddy I escaped and take your beating—and I won't tell him that the girl who's been shacked up in your brother's flat for the past few days is a spy for Brigs. I bet he would love to know that his son has been fucking the enemy, giving away his secrets for a bit of pussy."

The beast inside me returned in an instant, much stronger than before. I knew what would happen if my father ever found out about Evelyn's involvement with Brigs—he wouldn't care that she'd switched sides. He wouldn't care that I loved her more than life itself. He would kill her.

Every cell in my body itched to give in to the intoxicating rage bubbling in my blood, the monster snarling viciously to destroy the threat to my beloved. He dared threaten her—he *dared*.

"Or even better—how much is she worth to you? I saw the googly eyes you were giving her in that park. Perhaps we should be discussing the terms of your surrender? Unless you want to see the little tramp get butchered by your own father, of course."

My blood pounded in my ears like a war drum, drowning out all sense until everything was darkness.

The monster demanded pain.

And I obeyed.

---

*"MARCUS."*

The vaguely familiar voice penetrated through the shroud of fury, pulling me back up from the void as if hooking me with a line of clarity.

"Marcus, come back to me." Warmth seeped through my shirt to my skin where a soft hand touched me.

I blinked, my vision, still edged by blackness, slowly returning along with my conscience. My heart was hammering in my chest, my breathing ragged. I found myself kneeling in a pool of blood. My brothers were nowhere to be seen—and neither was the hostage. The man who had threatened my Evelyn.

But the pool of blood led to an unrecognizable corpse, and I knew what had become of him.

"It's okay. You're okay. I'm here now."

She had come for me. She had come to pull me from the darkness.

Slowly, I turned my head and I saw her. She stood by my side, my own personal guardian angel. My Evelyn.

*Evelyn.*

I stared at her through the haze, at her worried face with the soft lips and her full figure. Everything about her was warmth and light, and I needed her more than the air I breathed.

She made a squeaky little noise of surprise when I got to my feet and grabbed her face between my palms, but it was swallowed by the heated kiss I pressed to her lips. Sparks of elation and need fired from where our lips met all the way down through my body to my cock, already stiff and heavy between my legs. I ripped my lips from hers and pressed my mouth to her throat, moaning with the taste of her warm skin. My hands slid down her body and *tore,* and then the warm, full softness of her breasts spilled into my palms.

*Yes.*

"Marcus—*oh.*" Her voice broke off in a soft moan when I buried my mouth in the full globes, a nipple slipping in between my lips as if seeking the warmth of my tongue of its own accord. When I suckled deeply, she cried out and buried her hands in my hair.

There was nothing in the world but her. Nothing but her body and the overwhelming need to drown my darkness in her light until all the anger and all the horror went away, like it always did in her embrace.

Still with my lips around her swollen nipple, I fumbled for the opening to her pants. They gave with a ripping sound, and a shudder went through her when my fingers slipped in between her thighs, seeking entry to the core of her being. The core of her light.

"Marcus, stop," she breathed, her voice hitching a little when I switched to her other breast, sucking the nipple into my mouth with the same desperation as my hand pressed up between her legs. "We can't do this now."

I moaned against her breast, the sound as broken as my mind. I couldn't stop. I couldn't, or the darkness would consume me again until there was nothing but a shell left. But I couldn't hurt her, either.

I forced my mouth from her breasts and pressed my face in against her neck, breathing heavily from the sheer force it took to obey. Her scent—of honey and woman and *Evelyn*—filled my nostrils and fanned my desire to the point of physical pain. "I need you. Please, Evelyn. I need you. It hurts so much."

"Oh, Marcus," she whispered, and this time her voice was filled with pity—and love.

I kissed her because I couldn't stop myself. Even now, even when I was less than human, less than nothing, she loved me.

Her arms wound tightly around my neck until I pulled back. Then she took my hand and moved it back down between her thighs. When my fingers found her heat, her eyes fluttered closed and she sighed softly.

Relief mixed with my need, and I groaned. She was wet. She wanted me.

I ripped her pants so I could spread her thighs apart and rubbed my palm the full length of her slit, shuddering as warm slickness coated my skin. *Yes,* this was it. This was what my entire being yearned for—had yearned for since the first time the monster appeared. *Evelyn.*

She yelped when I spun her around and pressed her up against the wall, but she didn't resist. Only arched her hips backward, inviting me in.

*Yes, yes, yes!*

I ripped my jeans in my desperation to get to her, and then there was nothing between us, nothing to stop me from finding what I longed for so desperately.

Evelyn's cry was sharp when I seated myself in her tight heat, but the rush of blood in my ears blocked it out as her soft flesh clenched around me.

*"God!"* I roared as every cell in my body burned with completion. This was it—this was how it was meant to be, how I could finally find my soul again. Inside my beloved, inside her light.

I grabbed her hips and pulled almost all the way out before my need for her forced me back in. And again. The sharp spikes of pleasure every time I bottomed out in her nearly tore my mind apart, but it was a blissful sort of insanity. All I wanted was to lose myself in her until all that remained of me was the part of my heart she had saved.

*"Evelyn. I love you. I love you."*

I took her without thought for anything but the relief of finally being with the woman who was meant to be mine, my gasped confessions of love accentuated by her responding cries and the wet sounds of her sex swallowing my cock.

When I finally came inside of her, filling her with my essence in pulsing spurts, it was as if she drained the darkness from my mind as well.

For a long, blissful time, there was nothing but the perfect feeling of her soft body in my arms and her still-quivering pussy around my slowly deflating cock. Nothing but peace and light as my sanity slowly returned and the monster disappeared back to the depths.

It lasted until I opened my eyes and saw the woman I loved pressed up against the dank basement wall beneath me, her body shaking with her silent tears.

# TWENTY-ONE

## MARCUS

My heart pounded in my chest, but it was an oddly dull sensation. Like it was muted by the sense of falling, of the walls closing in around me.

I had hurt her. *Hurt* her. My Evelyn.

Slowly, moving as gently as I could, I pulled out of her.

She groaned when my cock slipped from her swollen entrance, and the sound cut through the numbness like a knife.

I'd been wrong. All these years, I had been so wrong. There wasn't a monster living in my chest, taking over my conscience when the darkness closed in.

*I* was the monster. All the time. With every fiber of my being.

I hurt her.

She remained leaning against the wall, her sides still moving rapidly from her gasps for air.

I knelt down behind her and slid my hands in between her folds, opening her up again. Everything in my brain screamed at me to get away from her, to never touch her again, but I couldn't do that--I had to make sure I hadn't caused any serious damage to her body. I had to know there wasn't any internal bruising. Or bleeding.

Her soft little sex was swollen and flushed red, but only my semen dripped out of her still quivering channel when I opened her. The proof of our coupling made a trickle of desire travel down my spine, and my cock give a half-hearted attempt at rising again.

"What are you doing?" she murmured, her voice drugged and hoarse. Had she been screaming while I took her? Had she screamed at me to stop?

The wave of nausea in my stomach intensified, making my cock fall again. I let go of her slick folds and got to my feet again, looking around for something to cover her with. I'd ruined her clothes in my desperation to get inside of her, and she didn't need to suffer the indignity of being dragged through the house for everyone to see what she had been put through. In my hands.

There was nothing but broken body parts, blood and the splintered leftovers of the chair our attacker had sat on in the small cell.

I unbuttoned my own shirt, the only piece of either of

our clothing that had made it through somewhat unscathed and held it out to her.

Evelyn wrinkled her nose at the blood spatters on the fabric, but she took it anyway. She was so small compared to me it came down well past her mid thighs.

"Come," I said to her when she gave me a careful look, as if she didn't know what to do now. "I will take you up to Mira. You'll be safe with her."

Evelyn grimaced, her eyes darting to the floor between us and the door. Some of the blood had formed a pool in front of it.

Of course she didn't want to walk through a man's fresh blood.

Without a word I reached out and lifted her up, biting back a groan when my wounds gave sharp shocks of pain. I had undoubtedly burst more than a few stitches when I killed Brigs' man, and fucking Evelyn like a beast likely hadn't helped.

I relished the pain as I stepped over the blood with Evelyn in my arms. I deserved pain—and so much more.

*I hurt her.*

I bit down on the wave of despair and self-loathing that washed over me as I made my way out of the basement and up the stairs with the woman who should have been my bride in my arms.

The door to the room Evelyn shared with Mira was open, and I could hear Blaine's quiet voice from within. Rob was nowhere to be seen, but he didn't need to be there as long as Blaine was present. My older brother would never in a million years let anything happen to his little family. Nor would he hurt them himself.

Both Mira and Blaine looked up when I stepped through the door, both with a look of mild concern on their faces.

"You all right, love?" Blaine asked.

"Oh. Yeah," Evelyn said. A faint blush touched her cheeks when she realized we had company, and shame ate at my gut. She shouldn't have to bear the humiliation of others knowing what I'd done to her, but I didn't have any other choice. I put her down next to the bed and turned to Blaine.

"Can I speak with you?"

"Sure," he said, giving Evelyn another glance before he followed me outside the room, closing the door behind him.

"I need a favor," I said, not letting him ask any of the questions I could see written across his face. "You said you had an out for Mira and Aidan?"

Blaine nodded once. "I do."

"I need Evelyn out of here. Tonight. For good. Can I count on you?"

He sighed and ran his fingers through his black hair. "You know neither I nor the twins will ever repeat what he said about her. She's safe here."

"Can I count on you?" I repeated, my voice tight from the tension in my body.

"What happened, Marcus?" he said, folding his arms across his chest. "Is it because she saw you... ah, *hulking out?*"

"I *hurt* her!" It wasn't quite a shout, but the sound of my shame spoken out loud still seemed to echo through my head until it filled the air. I buried my face in my hands and slumped against the wall, my muscles finally giving up their ability to keep me upright. "I hurt her, and she needs to get far, far away from me and all this shit so no one can ever harm her again. Especially me."

"Marcus..." Blaine sounded more than a little hesitant at my confession, but he gripped my shoulder and gave it what would have been a comforting squeeze had I had the ability to feel anything but pain and regret. "Are you sure you actually *hurt*-hurt her? She looks fine—or as fine as anyone can look after having walked in on one of your little massacres. And..." He sighed, and I could practically hear him steeling himself to force the words out. "Look, I know falling in love is... it's fucking brutal. Trust me, I get it. But mate, that girl stayed with you every minute of every day you were in the hospital. She switched sides for you, risking Brigs' wrath. We get one chance at true love. *One.* And the way you two look at each other... I'm pretty sure she's it for you. Do you really want to give up on her? Because if I use my connections to make her disappear— she's gone. For good. There won't be any second chances."

Another kind of pain made it through the fog of self-hatred, making my resolve flicker for a single moment. I knew, without a shadow of a doubt, that if I gave up Evelyn I would give up the only tie I'd ever found to my humanity. She was the only one who had ever been capable of making the darkness resign, the only one to pull me out of the depths of my black insanity.

Losing her would finally break my weak grasp on the parts of my soul I could ever have called good.

But there wasn't anything I wouldn't sacrifice for Evelyn. Even my own soul.

"I'm sure," I said, pushing down the cry of denial threatening to escape my throat. "She deserves to find love with someone who isn't a monster."

# TWENTY-TWO

EVELYN

"Are you all right?"

I looked up at Mira from my perch on the bed, not entirely sure how to answer her well-meaning question.

Specifically because my entire body was still throbbing from sexual exertion, and here I was, sitting half-naked in the company of a woman I'd seen only once before. I clutched Marcus' shirt tighter around my body and tried my best to suppress my embarrassed flush.

"Yeah. Thanks. Just a little..." Sweaty? Sticky? Still emotionally wrought from the intimate bond I'd shared with the man who'd dumped me with his sister-in-law minutes after the most intense sex of my life? There just really wasn't any way to finish that sentence, so I didn't even try.

"Ah, the Steel men," Mira said lightly as she walked over to the big, wooden wardrobe and began pulling out clothes. "Very intense. Not very good at easing a girl down to Earth after. Do you like navy blue? I think we're roughly the same size, aren't we?"

I looked at the simple, but elegant dress she was holding out and could have kissed her. "Navy blue is perfect. Thank you." To be fair, any color would have been fine if it meant I didn't have to spend the rest of my time in the Steel patriarch's house wearing Marcus' bloody shirt and ripped panties.

She smiled and handed me the dress, along with panties and gray woolen tights. "There's an en-suite if you want to freshen up a bit."

"Yeah, that would be good," I mumbled. A quick shower wouldn't be the worst of ideas, so I disappeared into the adjoining bathroom and turned on the shower.

If I'd had my way, I would have currently been curled up with Marcus somewhere where it was just the two of us and we could bask in the afterglow. Even the first time we'd made love, when he'd lost control and fucked me like a wild beast, it hadn't been as emotionally volatile as this time. This time had been... I didn't have words for what it had been, but I knew in the depths of my soul that I would never be the same.

The sex had been rough and the stench of blood littering the air hadn't exactly set the most romantic mood, and yet I had connected with my lover more deeply than I'd ever imagined possible. It had been just him and me, just the insurmountable need he had for me, and my longing to quell all the pain I knew was warring inside of him as he unleashed his agony with every thrust and every groan.

My heart skipped a beat as I remembered how fully he had surrendered himself to me in those moments of passion. I hadn't known it was possible to be that close to another human being, but he had shown me differently.

The sheer elation of knowing that I was loved and wanted and needed by the man my heart had fallen for without ever asking permission was the biggest gift of my life.

I'd sobbed like a baby once it was done, too overwhelmed with emotion and bliss to put into words what he meant to me.

Something I intended on rectifying the second he came back from whatever it was he was doing.

It was ironic, really. When Blaine had come into the room where Mira and I were waiting and said Marcus had "lost it" on the hostage, I'd rushed down to the basement—despite his attempt at stopping me—intent on saving Marcus from the nightmares I knew would follow if he lost control.

I hadn't given Brigs' man a second thought, hadn't cared about his life at all—and when I walked into the room and saw his mangled corpse, all my empathy had been with the hunched-up man with blood on his hands who'd been sobbing in the corner, oblivious to the world.

I'd tried to resist the pull between us from day one

because I didn't want any more part of the violence in the underworld than what Brigs had already forced me to participate in. Had thought being with a man who murdered people as part of his job would make me resent and fear him.

And yet, when it came down to it, it didn't matter. All that mattered was that he'd needed me, and I needed to be with him.

Even now, I didn't have much empathy for the man who had tried to kill Marcus and I, not even after how gruesome his end was. He'd tried to take away the man I loved. He deserved everything that came to him.

I walked out of the shower dressed in Mira's clothes, and found her sitting on the bed with Aidan in her arms and Blaine leaning against one of the bedposts.

"You called it, we are exactly the same size," I said and did a twirl before shooting Blaine a teasing smile. "Maybe the twins are right and you guys do, in fact, have a type."

The frown on both their faces made my smile falter. "What?"

"Marcus is waiting for you in the hallway," Blaine said, and something in his tone made my stomach drop.

"Is something wrong?" I asked, walking toward the door before I even knew my feet were moving. "Is it your dad?"

He just shook his head, and I didn't have time to stay and grill him—not if Marcus needed me.

He was waiting a few yards down the hallway, still

shirtless and with his hands pushed down the front of his jeans pockets. His face was as dark and broody as ever, and the churning in my gut clenched at the pain in his eyes.

"What's going on?" I asked as I stopped in front of him. I reached out to touch his bare arm, but he moved out of my reach before I could touch him.

Confused, I looked up into his stormy eyes. "Marcus, what's the matter?"

"I've talked with Blaine, and he has agreed to use his connections to send you out of the country. Tonight," he said, turning his face so he was no longer returning my gaze.

"I don't understand," I said, frowning at his words as much as the cold distance in his voice. "I thought you were staying here to fight with your family?"

"I am," he said. "You're going alone. Once you get on the plane, no one will be able to find you again. Not Brigs, not Blaine. Not me. I'll give you some starting capital so you can begin a new life somewhere else."

"But..." The clenching in my gut turned to lead as his words slowly began to sink in. I stared at him, willing it to all be a misunderstanding even as my shocked brain finally took in why he was so cold. He was leaving me. "But what about us?"

"There is no us," he said, an angry slant to his mouth. "And there never will be. Rob is waiting down in the driveway to take you to the airport. You're getting a ticket out of this life—out of all the violence and the crime. It's what you wanted, right from the start. I suggest you take it."

"Marcus..." I wanted to say something else, demand that he explain why he was doing this, why he had lied to me, but I couldn't force the words out. All I could do was stand there and stare at the man I'd given my soul, the man I'd trusted with everything I was as my heart broke into a million pieces.

He didn't want me, after all.

"Goodbye, Evelyn," he said, and then he turned around and walked down the hall, down the stairs, and out of my life.

I don't know how long I stood there, numb from shock and pain with tears trickling down my cheeks, but when I finally regained the ability to move it was like a layer of ice had closed around me. It was thin and brittle, but it made me able to walk down the stairs and out of the mansion to the waiting car.

He was right. This was what I'd wanted—a ticket out of London and the criminal hell I'd been wrapped up in for the past year and a half.

And if nothing else, that was what Marcus Steel had given me.

Even if the price was much higher than I'd ever wanted to pay.

"Can we drive by my flat on the way, please?" I asked Rob as I climbed into the backseat and shut the door behind me. "I need my passport."

"Everything's taken care of," he said, handing me a thick brown envelope before he turned the keys in the ignition of the sleek Lexus. "New identity, new passport, money. You'll be an entirely new woman once you walk into Heathrow."

I let my fingers slide over the envelope and felt the lumps inside. One of them felt like it was the size of a passport, and a couple of the others like rolls of money. An entirely new woman, huh? Well, at least that sounded good, because I couldn't stand to be the one I currently was for much longer.

"Wait for me!"

I jolted when the passenger door opposite me was

ripped open and Mira shoved a gurgling toddler through and into my arms before she followed, slamming the door shut behind her. "Go, quickly now, before Blaine realizes I've left the room."

Rob stared at her in the rear view mirror, mouth agape. "Absolutely not! Get back inside, before he sees us and skins me alive!"

"Oh, don't be so dramatic," Mira huffed even as she ducked down so no one from the house would be able see her. "We're with you, it's perfectly safe. And I'll deal with Blaine. Just drive, Rob. The sooner you get us there, the sooner you can get us back again."

He stared at her for a moment longer, and then let out a string of profanity as he set the car in gear and pulled out of the driveway. "I miss the days when you were scared of him."

"So does he," she said with a cheerful smile before she straightened up in the seat and reached out to grab Aidan again. Then she turned to me, tilting her head a little.

"What happened in the basement, Evelyn?"

I shook my head. "Doesn't matter now."

"Of course it matters. Before he went down there, you two were getting married, and now he's sending you away? Did he hurt you?"

I frowned. "No, of course not. He... we... I thought I comforted him. I thought... I thought everything was good. But I guess I was wrong."

"Hm," she said, still with that head-tilt that made me

feel like she was trying to analyze me. "Well, I might not always understand what goes on in that head of his, but I do know that Marcus loves you. More than he probably knows how to express. All the Steel brothers... they're pretty damaged. They had a rotten childhood, and to put it blatantly, it's really messed them up. Especially Marcus. He's always been so withdrawn, hardly ever spoke. Until you showed up.

"Evelyn, I don't know what happened or why he's suddenly decided the best thing is to send you away, but I promise you it's not because he doesn't love you, or whatever idiotic thing he told you to make you give up without a fight. Knowing him, it's probably some misguided attempt at protecting you. They're big on that—protecting the people they love—and sometimes it comes across in less than ideal ways."

I shook my head, willing my tears to stay put. "You didn't see him. He meant what he said. If he loved me, he wouldn't have sent me away. You don't do that to someone you care about. I learned that early on in life."

She gave me a sad little smile and shifted her baby so she could put a hand on my arm. "You have to do what you think is right for you, I get that. Forgive me for being pushy about it—I have a soft spot for my brother-in-law, and the only time I've seen him look happy was with you. As long as you are one hundred percent sure that this is the end of the road for you two, then getting out is probably the smartest thing you can do."

I bit my lip and nodded, not trusting my voice to hold as I watched her bounce the toddler when he started fussing. He had the same dark hair and gray eyes as his father and uncle, and looking at him made an achy spasm cut through me. it was what Marcus said he wanted with me—a baby and a future. And I... I'd let myself want it, too. Looking at Aidan made the longing for everything I'd never have well up, sharp and painful. I turned away and looked out the window at the passing traffic instead.

Soon, I would be able to forget I'd let myself believe that life came with happy endings for people like me.

Mira didn't try to broach the subject of Marcus again, but she kept her hand on my arm for the rest of the drive.

When Rob pulled over in Heathrow she gave me a one-armed hug and the same, sad smile as before. "Good luck, Evelyn."

"Thanks," I said, feeling like I should say some more but not knowing what. "You too. With... everything."

"We'll be fine," she said, her smile turning somewhat more determined. "There's nothing the Steels won't do for their family."

I nodded, clutching my envelope in one hand before I climbed out of the car.

It was an odd feeling of loss, watching them drive off. Something about knowing that they were on their way back to fight for the family that had almost been mine made a fresh wave of grief flood through my system, and I steeled myself against the press of tears.

Irritated with myself for dwelling on what could have been I tore open the envelope to get a look at my new identity.

Apart from cash and a passport with a photo of me along with the name Emily Brisbane, there was an awful lot of documents in the envelope.

I leafed through them, finding a plane ticket and a pre-paid hotel room in Chicago. I almost closed the envelope then, intent on looking through everything else when I was on the plane, when my eyes caught sight of another plane ticket, this one with the name Eleonore Brisbane on it.

I frowned. It was for tomorrow rather than this evening, and instead of leaving from Heathrow it went from Chicago to California.

Quickly, I looked through the rest of the documents, looking for an explanation.

When I found it, my legs nearly gave out from underneath me.

Fumbling, I dropped down on the concrete wall separating the pavement from the trolleys as I stared at the piece of paper in my shaking hand.

It outlined detailed treatment plans for advanced Alzheimer trials at UCLA for one Mrs. Eleonore Brisbane.

I recognized the name of the program. A year and a half ago, when my mum first got diagnosed, I had frantically looked up any and all possible ways to cure it, and found none—apart from a newly commenced closed-trial program in California, which showed promising results but were still years off being made available to the public.

And, I'd been told by the kind doctor who had diagnosed my mother, even when it did become available to the public, it would likely be another decade before it would be available through the NHS. It would be far, far too expensive to pay privately, even if my mother's memory would be salvageable so far into the disease.

And yet here I sat, with a document that would let Mrs. Eleonore Brisbane undertake treatment no one on the planet had access to.

If it went well, someday I could potentially get my mother back.

Marcus had given me a chance for my mother to return to me.

At the bottom of the treatment arrangement was a small note attached with a paper clip. It simply read: *I need you to be happy.*

It was an interesting feeling, going from so much grief to the shock of my discovery, and then elation so intense my mind struggled to grasp it. But in the mix of confusion, one thing became increasingly clear the longer I stared at Marcus' note: he still cared for me. Very much. Not even a guilty conscience for going back on his promises of a future together would make someone spend the kind of resources this trial would cost for someone they didn't care about.

And I had let him go without a fight.

I'd been too scared of the hurt from his rejection to stop and question him on his sudden change of heart, too consumed in my own pain to stand my ground and demand an explanation.

Was Mira right? Was this some idiotic attempt at protecting me?

I didn't know, but as I stared at the envelope he'd prepared for me, I knew that I could never be sure until I'd talked to him and demanded that he explain what had happened to make him change his mind.

Could I really live with the knowledge that I'd given up on a man who would go to these lengths for me, without trying my damnedest first?

No. No, I could not.

A refreshing wave of resolve burned through the numb grief, and I got to my feet. Even if he no longer felt anything for me, if this truly was just a parting gift, then I was going to make him look me in the eye and explain everything, and not just ship me off because it was easier that way.

I rented out a safety box in the airport, leaving most of the contents of the envelope minus some money for a cab behind, and then went out to the taxi ramp.

Marcus Steel might think he was done with me, but I wasn't done with him. Not yet.

THE SOLITARY HOUSE on the country road outside of one of London's poshest suburbs was a looming block of quietude. There wasn't a single car parked up by the house as far as I could tell, and I frowned as I slipped the cab driver his payment and got out of the car.

Was tonight the big strike against Brigs?

Worry for Marcus fluttered in my belly as I began walking up the driveway. Surely Mira and Aidan would be inside, still guarded by Rob as Blaine had demanded. She would know when they would be back.

It was probably because of the darkness and the large, evergreen bushes lining the driveway that the twenty or more dark figures sneaking around from the back of the house in a hunched-over run didn't spot me as they made their way to the front door.

I stopped dead in my tracks, adrenaline snaking its way up my spine even before my brain managed to put two and two together.

Someone was trying to break into the Steel mansion while everyone was away. A lot of someones.

A sharp shock of panic lanced through the raw adrenaline.

Not everyone was away—Mira and Rob were inside, with the baby.

Rob might be a big, scary-looking mobster, but no way he could take on that many at a time.

My heart hammered in my chest, forcing me into action. I dove behind one of the bushes and dug out my phone, frantically scrolling through the contacts until I found Blaine's number.

I pressed "call", praying he would pick up.

The phone rang three times, and I feared my heart would leap out of my throat as the quiet buzz seemed to permeate the silent evening. If whoever was breaking in heard me and came looking, I was done for.

But if I didn't call, Mira and Aidan would be dead.

When the call connected, I didn't wait for Blaine to answer.

"Blaine, it's Evelyn. Someone's breaking into your dad's house. There's at least twenty of them. Come back quick," I whispered as loudly as I dared.

An inventive curse hissed back at me from the other end.

"*God dammit, I knew it was a fucking trap,*" Blaine's voice crackled through my phone. "*Get out of there now, we're coming.*"

"But Mira and Aidan are in there, I have to get to them," I protested, even though I had no idea how on Earth I was going to take on a group of probably-armed criminals. "Is there a backdoor, or—"

"*Evelyn, listen to me, get out of there now. Mira and Aidan are safe, they're not there, and if those men catch you—*"

I didn't hear what else he said, because just then someone clamped their hand around my mouth from behind, pulling me backwards through the bush. I shrieked and flailed wildly, but the sound was absorbed by the meaty hand pressing painfully tight against my lips. A hard slap against my hand sent my phone flying into the dirt.

"Well, well, what do we have here?" a harsh voice growled into my ear. "A filthy Steel spy, hiding in the begonias?"

I bit down, hard, on my attacker's palm and kicked backwards, aiming for his shins.

The man cursed and released his grip on my mouth long enough for me to suck in a lungful of air.

"Marcus!"

My scream rang through the night, but I didn't have time to ponder why it was the name of my ex-lover and not his brother I cried out for before a sharp blow to my temple made pain explode in my head and the world flicker as it went blank.

# TWENTY-FOUR

## MARCUS

I had never experienced the kind of sick fear that crept up through my chest and wrapped an icy cold hand around my throat as Blaine cussed into the phone moments after calling Evelyn's name.

"Blaine," I said, clutching at the steering wheel of the car I'd been driving—up until it became obvious who Blaine was talking to. "Where is she?"

"Dad's house," he said, hanging up on the call before he quickly pressed in another number and held the device back up to his ear. "This whole fucking mission is a trap. Hello?" The last word he spoke into the phone, his attention leaving me, but I didn't care. I'd heard enough.

Tires squealing, I set the car back into gear and ripped it around, stepping on the speeder until my foot touched the floor.

*Brigs has Evelyn.*

Flashes of what I'd done to his nephew made me grit my teeth to keep from crying out with terror. If his lackey had known what she meant to me, Brigs did too—and he wouldn't hesitate to hurt her to get back at me.

*Oh God, Evelyn, why did you come back?*

Beside me, Blaine was shouting instructions into his phone, but my focus was purely on the road ahead. I didn't care what they were planning, nor what consequences tonight would have. All I knew was that Evelyn needed me and I had to get to her before it was too late.

When we pulled up in front of the house it was still cloaked in darkness, but I could make out shapes moving inside the windows, watching. We were expected.

"Marcus, wait. If you go in without backup, he'll kill you," Blaine said, putting a hand on my arm as I unclipped the seatbelt.

"I don't care if he kills me," I hissed, climbing out of the car before Blaine could stop me.

The passenger side door opened, and he crawled out. "Marcus, for fuck's sake, you crazy bastard, you won't help her by committing suicide! Just wait for five fucking minu—"

I shoved past him and walked up the driveway with long strides, hands lifted above my head. Hopefully she was still alive. Hopefully Brigs would be satisfied with me instead of her.

I didn't stop until I was a few yards from the front door, hands still above my head.

"Gerald!" I shouted, clenching my fists above my head to keep myself from storming through the door. The snarling monster in my chest was roaring to be set free, but I knew that if I gave in, Brigs would kill Evelyn before I could ever get to her. So for the first time in my life, I kept control of the monster, even though everything in me begged to unleash it.

A short moment later the front door opened, and there he stood. Holding Evelyn in front of him like a shield, a gun pointed at her temple.

"Well, well. If it isn't the murderer himself," Brigs said, his voice as icy as ever. "And what can I do for you this fine evening? Let me guess: you're here for the little whore?"

"Don't speak about her," I snarled, unable to keep a hold of my fury at the blatant display of disrespect to the woman whimpering in his grasp.

"Oh, that's funny, you think you get to make demands?" he chuckled. "You murder my nephew, my heir, after this dumb cunt betrays me, and you try to tell me who I can speak about? No, son, that's not how this is going to play out. You see..." Brigs tapped Evelyn's temple lightly with the gun, making her cringe. "I was planning on ransacking your father's home for valuables before setting it on fire while you were all off dying in the trap I've so painstakingly laid out for you... and then who do I find in the flowerbeds, ruining all my hard work and carefully laid plans? My former employee! So I do hope you understand that I'm a little displeased with Miss Embry's performance these past few weeks, and a stern talking to is inevitable."

I gritted my teeth as my gaze swept over Evelyn, trying to determine the best way to make Brigs surrender her. I'd never been the diplomat in the Family, and right now every instinct in my body was screaming to throw myself at my enemy and save the woman who had claimed my heart.

"Take me instead," I said. "Do with me what you want. Just let her go."

"Oh, so my informants were right?" he said, that cold chuckle once more ringing through the driveway. "You did fall for the piece of arse I sent to ensnare you? Ah, you Steel boys, so bloody predictable. Play into your mummy issues, and you fall like dominoes. It would be pitiful, really, if it wasn't because you were all such a smug bunch of pricks. You get that from your father, of course. You've always been his spitting image, inside and out."

I bit the inside of my cheeks until i could taste blood, the urge to tear his flesh from his bones nearly insurmountable now.

"Please." It came out as a hoarse whisper. "My family will be here soon. I will make a better hostage."

"Will you, though?" Brigs said, tilting his head a little. "Do I bank on William Steel loving his most infamous son enough to watch in silence as I burn his empire to the ground and once and for all prove to the rest of the underworld that the Steels are done for? Or do I keep the girl and get you to plead my case and, if necessary, protect me from your own father and brothers? I think I might just like my chances better with dear Evelyn here as my trump card. Or what do you think, Evelyn? Does he love you enough to kill his own family if they attack us?"

"Go to hell," she hissed, murderous rage clear in her voice even as her defiance ended in a pained whimper when he yanked her hair backward.

"I think that's a yes," Brigs said, smiling with false cheerfulness as his gaze focused behind me. "I guess we're about to find out, huh, boy?"

I heard them behind me then, fast feet on the driveway and rustling in the evergreen bushes surrounding the lush gardens.

My Family had come.

"What you you doing, Gerald?" my father's voice came from somewhere behind me, sounding more conversational than angry at finding his long-time friend-turned-traitor on his doorstep. "You know we've got you outmanned and outgunned. This is folly."

"Do you, though? Marcus, perhaps you want to plead my case, hmm?" Brigs said. When I hesitated, he jabbed Evelyn with the gun once more, and I had to clutch my hands until the nails dug into my palms and drew blood to stop myself from attacking him.

"Let him do what he wants," I ground out, turning to

my father. "He can have the fucking house, and whatever else he desires."

"Oh, for heaven's sake!" My father said, looking crestfallen. "Is it the bloody girl? You want us to give up everything for some stray bitch you've dragged in off the street? And you," he said, turning to Brigs. "I can only assume you think I've gone soft in my old days if you think this desperate ploy is going to work."

"Oh, I don't know," Brigs said, an unpleasant smile curving his lips. "Ask your son if he's going to let you attack me. I do have his *beloved*, after all."

My father sighed, an exasperated sound. "Gerald... for old time's sake I'm giving you this *one* opportunity to tell your men to lay down their weapons before I order mine to kill every last one of you. I concede, what happened to your nephew was unfortunate, but you *did* try to steal information from my son."

Brigs' eyes narrowed. "No deal, old friend. Tonight, your reign ends. *Fred!*"

I braced, ready for an attack, but at first, nothing happened. Then orange light lit up on the sky from the back of the house, a *whooshing* sound ripping through the night.

My father's face contorted in anger when the flames licking at the roof became visible in the next moment. "You are going to regret this!"

"Dad, *no!*" I saw his intention in his eyes before he

vocalized it and rushed forward, a hand stretched out. "*Don't!* He'll kill her!"

"Get out of the way!" he sneered, and then raised his voice. "*Attack!*"

I didn't pause to think. When his order cracked through the air I lunged, my desperation mixing with fury and carrying me forward. My fist impacted with his face before anyone could react, taking him to the ground as dirt and gravel flew around us.

"She's my fiancée!" I yelled as I tackled him. "I *love* her! But you don't care, do you? You don't fucking care about any of us! I hate you! I *hate* you!"

I wasn't aware of the words I was slinging at him, nor the tears—I only felt the deep-seated hatred and anguish I'd carried for this man for so many years finally erupting in an explosion from the deepest, darkest part of my soul. I swung at him, breaking his nose, but before I could do any more damage a sharp kick to my side right where I'd been shot knocked me off him. I grunted from the searing agony and rolled several feet before I landed on my back, momentarily stunned from the pain.

Wesley's face came into focus above me. He was holding a gun, aiming it at my chest. "You shouldn't have done that," he said, his voice oddly businesslike. As if in slow motion I saw him release the safety, shaking his head as he did as if tutting at a disobedient child.

But before he could pull the trigger, Wesley froze, his eyes widening before they glazed over and he tipped backwards like a falling tree-trunk, the gun dropping limply from his hands. Two red holes sullied his dark-clad chest.

"You all right?" One of the twins stood above me, a gun still in his hand. He reached the other down and pulled me up.

"Evelyn?" I asked instead of answering, swirling around to look for her. My father's estate had erupted into mayhem. Guns were firing all around us, making bullets fly and men groan, but there was no sign of my beloved. Nor Brigs.

"Brigs got her. Inside," my brother said, forcing me down to a crouch behind a plant pot. "We'll get her, we just need a pla—*Marcus!*"

I ignored his shout as I ran for the stairs, pulling my own gun out from my inner pocket as I dodged out of the way for Brigs' men. When I got to the door one of them finally turned my way, gun aimed, but I got to him first. He fell to the ground with a bullet between the eyes, and so did the man inside who tried to take me down when I came crashing through the door.

Inside, the roar of the fire spreading through the house was deafening, and smoke was starting to seep through the cracks to the entryway.

I looked around, my pulse pounding so hard in my ears it nearly drowned out the crackling pops from the fire consuming my childhood home. *Where are you, Evelyn?*

I saw the smoke billowing thicker from the left side of the house and bolted to the other end, running as fast as I could despite my wounds. If Brigs had her, he would be moving away from the worst of the fire, trying to buy himself more time as his men fought ours outside to clear a path for him.

I came to a stop when I tried to push through the kitchen door and found it locked.

*Finally.*

I kicked the door in, satisfaction surging through me as it flew off its hinges and shattered on the black and white tiles.

Brigs was standing against the far wall, his hand still clutched in Evelyn's hair and the gun pointed up at her chin.

"Well done on taking your father down, son," he said, but the mocking smile on his lips was tense. "Now be a good kid and slide your gun over here and you can have your girl back."

I pulled my lip up in a silent snarl, not taking my eyes off him.

He arched an eyebrow. "Do you really want to test me? It's a stressful situation—my finger might just slip, and then pretty Evelyn won't be so pretty anymore."

Seething, I bent to slide my weapon across the floor toward him. I wanted to kill him more than I'd wanted to kill anyone since I saw Leo torture Evelyn, but I knew I had to restrain myself or she would pay for my mistakes.

Quick as a snake, Brigs bent to pick up my gun, releasing his hold on Evelyn. My heart gave a spasm of pent-up relief, but it was quashed the moment he turned my gun back on her, his own now aimed at me.

"Ah, there we go. That's *much* better," he said, the coldness in his eyes flickering for something darker. "You stupid son of a bitch, did you really think I was going to simply give you back the girl who betrayed me? Who you murdered my nephew for? Love really does make you blind, huh? And dumb. No, this is how we're going to do this..." He pushed Evelyn with the muzzle of my gun, making her stagger a foot to his side so he could keep her at arm's distance. "You get to choose, Marcus. One of you can live. The other... I'll shoot. So what's it going to be? Your own life, or the traitorous slut you fucked while thinking about your mother? And before you answer, may I remind you that if you choose a noble death worthy of a Shakespearean tragedy, there's the small matter of your father. With you gone, you think he's going to let her live? The cunt who made his own son turn against him? Ah, decisions, decisions."

"Me. Kill me," I said, not hesitating for more than a second. He was right about my father—he would take his fury with me out on Evelyn if I was not there to protect her, but I knew without a shadow of doubt that Blaine would take care of her. He would put her on a plane and she and her mother could live a happy life in America, forgetting all the horrors. Forgetting me.

"Marcus, *no!*" Evelyn gasped, but Brigs only smiled his cruel smile, uncocking the gun trained on me.

I didn't look at him, choosing instead to keep my gaze locked on Evelyn. Even now, with her face twisted in fear, she was so unbelievably beautiful. And for a short moment in time, she had been mine.

"Goodbye, Evelyn," I said softly, touching my hand to my heart.

But instead of despair, her expression changed into anger so fierce it looked foreign on her delicate face. Faster than I'd thought she could move, she swung around and grabbed the barrel of the gun trained on her with one hand, smacking Brig's arm right in the elbow joint so hard I heard the crack from across the room.

He yelped, losing his grip on my gun as she ripped it from his numbed fingers and turned it around on him, holding it up with both hands.

He stared at her with his mouth open in shock, but she didn't hesitate. The room rang with the sound of first one, then two, and finally three shots as she put three bullets in his chest and stomach.

Still with that shocked expression plastered across his now frozen face, he slid to the ground with a thud. Dead.

# TWENTY-FIVE

EVELYN

I'd never killed a man before.

Of all the horrible things I'd done in the past year and a half, killing hadn't been among them. I'd always thought that taking another human being's life, however vile they were, would feel awful. But as I looked down at Brigs' blindly staring eyes, I felt nothing but relief. The man who had made my life hell for so long was finally dead.

"Evelyn." Strong arms wrapped around me, pulling me away from the sight of the bleeding body on the floor. "Are you hurt, my love?"

"No," I mumbled groggily, resting my head against Marcus' shoulder. My body, apparently deciding that as long as he was there it no longer had to keep me upright, went limp with exhaustion as adrenaline slowly seeped out of me, and I sagged in his arms.

"Just hold on a little longer. We need to get out of the

house," he said, and awareness returned as the smell of smoke registered in my nostrils once more.

I forced my limbs to take most of my weight, but Marcus kept an arm around my shoulders as he guided us through the outer wall of the house, supporting my wobbly legs for every step. When we reached the back of the house, the heat was unbearable and the smoke was getting thicker.

"We have to get out now," I coughed into my sleeve. My eyes stung and it was hard to see.

"Hold on," Marcus grunted. "We're at the back of the house now, less chance of getting shot." He released my shoulders, and the next moment, I heard the sound of breaking glass.

"Come on, Evelyn," he coughed, pulling on my coat. "Make sure you stick to the curtain."

Through the slits of my eyes, I could see he'd smashed in a window and pulled a curtain down to place over the frame so we could climb out without cutting ourselves to shreds.

The cold air was like a slap to the face when I tumbled through the open window and landed in the flower bed underneath it. I rolled over onto my hands and knees and coughed until all I could feel in my lungs was air.

That's when I noticed that Marcus was crouched next to me, gasping for air and holding his side, and a stab of fear shot through me, killing the momentary respite.

"Are you hurt?" I asked, reaching for him to try and find the source of his pain. He had to be all right. We hadn't gone through all of this for him not to be all right

"No," he managed to choke out. "Bastard kicked me in the side, burst some stitches. I'm fine."

He didn't look fine, but when he drew in a final, deep breath before moving into a crouch, some of my initial panic settled.

"We need to get out of here," I said, looking out from behind the large rosebush we were hiding behind. There weren't any combatants in this part of the garden, but shots were still being fired from the front part of the estate.

Marcus nodded. "Yeah, we—" His voice cut off abruptly as two shadow moved around the corner in a low run, and Marcus fumbled in his pocket for his gun—the gun still lying on the kitchen floor inside the burning building. Cursing, he pressed me back with his body, physically shielding me from the approaching figures.

"Marcus?" a low hiss sounded, and my heart skipped a beat from pure relief. *Blaine.*

"It's us," Marcus confirmed, his protective stance in front of me relaxing as he got to his legs. Seconds later I could make out both Blaine's and one of the twins' faces in the dark as they stopped in front of us.

"You both all right?" Blaine asked, eyes roaming over both his brother and my huddled-up form.

"Never better," I muttered.

"Brigs?"

"Dead," Marcus said, glancing at me, but he didn't elaborate. "Dad?"

"Still fighting, along with Louis. We've almost got them all now. It's a matter of minutes, so you two need to come with us. Right now. If Dad finds you, you're both dead."

WHEN I GOT out of the shower attached to the small hotel room Blaine had driven us to, Liam was in the final stages of stitching up Marcus' wounds, both men sitting on the bed while Blaine was messing with his phone by the room's single window.

"There," Liam said as he wrapped a clean bandage around Marcus' torso. "That should keep you from bleeding out the second the plane takes off, but you're gonna want to find a doctor when you land."

Marcus grunted noncommittally, and Liam turned his eyes on me. "If he doesn't do it, poke him in the side wound. A nice, hard jab should make him plenty compliant, yeah?"

I grimaced, but Liam just winked at me, his eyes sparkling with mischief despite the serious situation.

"Louis's managed to send Dad to Gatwick looking for you two, but it won't be long before he'll have freed enough men from dealing with Brigs to spread them to

Heathrow, too," Blaine said as he shoved his phone in his pocket and walked over to us, handing us each a ticket. "Your new flight leaves in a couple of hours, but Liam and I will need to get back to deal with Dad, lest he thinks we're revolting. Have you still got everything else Rob gave you, Evelyn?"

I nodded. "I took out a lock box at the airport."

"Clever girl." He offered me a small smile before his focus switched to Marcus, his smile fading. "I'll be in touch when it's safe to come home."

Marcus nodded, placing his hand on Blaine's shoulder. "Thank you."

"Anything for family," Blaine said softly, squeezing Marcus' shoulder in return. "Be safe."

"And you."

"Always." Blaine nodded at me, giving his brother one final look before he walked out of the hotel room. Liam didn't say anything, but he pulled first me and then Marcus into a tight hug before he followed Blaine out, shutting the door behind him.

I looked up at Marcus, clutching the ticket in my hands. "You're coming with me, right?"

He nodded, but the look of guilt on his face took away the rush of relief. "I'm sorry, Evelyn."

"For what?" I asked, genuinely baffled. Somehow, against all odds, we'd both made it out alive, and he was *sorry?*

"Everything," he said softly. "I wanted to give you a

new life, a free life. I never wanted you to experience a night like this."

I shook my head and turned so I could press myself against his body. He stiffened, as if he didn't know what to do.

"There's nothing to be sorry for. We're together—that's all that matters."

Marcus shook his head. "No, Evelyn. We're not. I can't..."

I gaped up at him as his voice trailed off, but instead of the expected pang of hurt, only anger bloomed in my chest.

"You can't what? Be with me? Love me? What, exactly, is it you think you can't, Marcus?"

He cringed and looked away from my fury. "You deserve so much better. I *hurt* you. I..."

I grasped him by the chin and pulled his face back so he couldn't look away. "Now you listen to me, Marcus Steel. What I deserve is to be *happy*. And loved. And for that to happen, you need to get over whatever it is you think is wrong with you so we can be together. I need you, don't you get it? *You.* You haven't hurt me, and you never will hurt me. All you've done, from the moment we met, is protect me and care for me. And all I want is to protect and care for you, too. I know we were meant to be together, with every part of my soul. So stop fighting it because you're afraid."

Marcus blinked, clearly stunned by my rant. "I... didn't hurt you? But... you cried."

I rolled my eyes—I just couldn't help it. "You mean in the basement? I cried because you finally let me in behind the darkness and it was the most raw and beautiful moment of my life. And then you went and ruined it by thinking you knew what was best for me instead of bloody *asking* me."

He stared at me for the longest time, seemingly taking forever to process what I'd said. But I'd had enough of waiting. Rising up on my tip-toes I wrapped my arms around his neck and pressed my lips to his, reveling in the warmth of his mouth as we kissed, long and gently.

"What about the monster?" he whispered against my lips when I pulled back for breath some time later. "The darkness. It's a part of me. Pretending like it's not is pointless. You deserve so much more than that."

I smiled and drew against him as he instinctively held me closer. "I kind of love your monster. Haven't you noticed that all it wants to do is protect you and the people you care about? I don't want *more* than what you are, Marcus, because you're already everything I could ever want and more."

He opened his mouth, but no words came out. Instead he just looked at me with clear amazement written across his impossibly handsome face.

"What?" I asked.

The gentlest of smiles spread slowly across his mouth,

lifting up the corners and making me gasp at the pure, unadulterated love shining from his silvery eyes. "I love you. From the first time I saw you, I've loved you. And I will love you with all that I am until the day I die."

I smiled back at him. "I'm glad, because I'm not letting anything come between us ever again. Not even you, you hear?"

The smile slipped off his face. "Loud and clear, my love. But I just have one question. It dawned on me I never asked you."

"Asked me what?" I said, frowning at his serious expression.

"Will you marry me?" Marcus grasped my hands and knelt down, wincing as he did. When he was resting on one knee, he looked back up at me, and the emotion in his eyes made my heart throb hard and fast behind my ribs as a grin spread on my face.

"You arse! You had me all worried!"

He simply smiled, stroking his thumbs across my knuckles in a gentle caress. "Will you?"

"Yes. I will marry you, Marcus."

TROUBLE

Read the twins' story in *Trouble*, book 3 in the Made &
Broken series.

## Trouble

*I share everything with my twin—every man I kill and every woman I fuck.*

## Audrey

If there is one thing I don't have time for, it's men. Especially not men six years my junior, with a wicked smile and abs for days. No self-respecting woman with career goals and bills to pay would fall for a guy like Liam Steel—he's everything I never wanted, with his easy laugh and complete disregard for rules.

He's not the man for me, I know he isn't. He's got secrets, and if I get too close they'll end up burning me alive.

So why can't I stay away?

## Liam

It was meant to be a harmless fling—she was *supposed* to be just another quick fuck before I was out the door. But Audrey Waits is so much more than I ever thought she'd be.

She's the one.

I should be happy I've found the woman I want to marry. After all, isn't that what everyone spends their entire life searching for? Their one true love.

Too bad I'll never get my Happily Ever After.

How can I, when being with me means she's marked for death?

## Louis

It was always Liam and me. Through every hit we've done, every woman we've fucked and every loss we've suffered, we've been left standing because we had each other's backs.

Then *she* showed up. The prissy little bird who's wrapped my twin around her finger, making him careless. Making him vulnerable.

In our business, you have a weakness, you're dead. And if there's one thing I won't survive, it's losing Liam.

So I'll protect him—even from himself, if I have to.

I'll make her think I'm him.

And then I'll *break* her.

She'll regret the day she fell in love with a Steel.

# TROUBLE - SNIPPET

## LOUIS

"Where are you off to?" I raised my eyebrows at my twin as he walked into the kitchen, wearing a pressed shirt and smart jeans. Not completely unusual attire for him, but he looked somehow... neater than usual. And he was fiddling with his cuff, like he usually did when he was nervous.

"Audrey's dad's birthday," he said with a grimace.

*Audrey.*

My stomach dropped with uncomfortable foreboding. The little prude he'd picked up from a pub a few weeks ago. I hadn't asked, but I knew that's where he'd been sleeping most nights this past week. With *her.*

This was the longest he'd ever been with a girl before—that either of us had, and I wasn't stupid. He liked her. Fuck, he was going to a goddamn family birthday with her now? He more than liked her.

Worry mixed with something else, something dark

and painful I didn't want to prod further twisted in my gut. We both knew we couldn't afford distractions right now, and getting attached to a bird was about the dumbest fucking thing he could have done. Soon as you cared for someone, they became a weakness. Just look at fucking Marcus—he'd only narrowly avoided death because he lost his head when his girl was in danger.

If that happened to Liam...

The dark thing in my gut clenched and snarled at the thought.

If that happened, I could lose him.

"You've been seeing her a lot lately," I said, keeping my tone casual.

He shot me a quick glance, and I could tell from the look in his eyes that I hadn't managed to hide my worry completely.

"Yeah. She's a good distraction."

"Mmhm," I hummed, not buying it for a second. Multiple birds were fine distractions—one was fucking trouble. "You in love with her?"

If I hadn't known him so well, I would have missed the millisecond his fingers froze against his cuff.

"Nah, it's nothing serious. Don't worry." He gave me a brilliant smile before he turned his back on me and headed to the hallway, grabbing his leather jacket on the way. "See you later!"

The front door slammed shut behind him, and I frowned into the silence that settled in our shared flat.

That was the first time my twin had ever lied to me.

---

I PARKED FAR ENOUGH AWAY from the door Liam had disappeared into that when he came back out again ten minutes later hand in hand with a woman, he didn't spot me. Not that he would have noticed much, the way he was looking down at her as if there was only the two of them in the entire fucking world.

The dark thing in my gut twisted when he stopped to brush a lock of her hair away from her forehead. The look on his face, then... of complete and utter worship. He loved her. He loved her the same way Blaine loved his wife, the same way Marcus loved the girl he threw everything away to be with.

It was like a mule-kick right in my sternum, and I had to clench my hands around the steering wheel until my knuckles turned white to keep myself from keeling over at the strength of the panic that tore through me at that look.

A tsunami of emotions warred inside that black pit in my gut, but at the root of it all was all-consuming, mind-numbing *fear*. Fear of losing the one person in this world that had kept me from giving in to the violence and despair that was our birthright. Fear of being left alone when she either got my twin killed, or if... I breathed deeply when the wave of jealousy so hot it burned my esophagus clawed its way to the surface.

If this was it for him, if that girl was to Liam what Mira was to Blaine, or Evelyn to Marcus... Then even if we somehow made it through the fight against our father, I would still lose him. It wouldn't be him and me against the world anymore. She would take my place, and I...

I knew I'd never survive that.

Continue reading in
TROUBLE

ALSO BY NORA ASH

MADE & BROKEN SERIES

Dangerous

Monster

Trouble

DEMON'S MARK SERIES

Branded

Demon's Mark

Prince of Demons

FERAL SERIES

Obsession

Despair

Torment

ALPHA SERIES

Taken

Masquerade

Mated

THE OMEGA PROPHECY

Ragnarök Rising

Weaving Fate

ANCIENT BLOOD SERIES

Origin

Wicked Soul

Debt of Bones*

DARKNESS SERIES

Into the Darkness

Hidden in Darkness

Shades of Darkness

Fires in the Darkness

WWW.NORA-ASH.COM